This book is due for return on or before the last date shown below.

Other titles by Pat Moon

Black Apples
Double Image
Nathan's Switch
The Spying Game

Red Apples
Do Not Read This Book
Do Not Read Any Further

ORCHARD BOOKS
96 Leonard Street, London EC2A 4XD
Orchard Books Australia
32/45-51 Huntley Street, Alexandria, NSW 2015
ISBN 1 84362 202 5
First published in Great Britain in 1997
First paperback publication in 1997
This edition published in 2003
Text © Pat Moon 1997
The right of Pat Moon to be identified as the author
of this work has been asserted by her in accordance with
the Copyright, Designs and Patents Act, 1988.
A CIP catalogue record for this book is available from the British Library.
1 3 5 7 9 10 8 6 4 2
Printed in Great Britain

Every effort has been made to source the songs cited in this book, but we could
not find any information to indicate that they were still in copyright to anyone.
If our findings were incorrect, please contact Orchard Books immediately

The Ghost of Sadie Kimber

Pat Moon

ORCHARD BOOKS

Laura would never forget her thirteenth birthday.
It was the day she tried to convince Nick.
Sadie was no joke. Sadie had taken over.
And Sadie was dangerous.

Chapter One

*Some ghosts seem to fade away. Others remain dormant for
many years and become reactivated by human company.*
THE HANDBOOK OF HAUNTINGS *by* O.M. PATON

Laura peered out of the shed window and pleaded, 'Come
on, someone. Find me.'

No one heard her. Though Mrs White, snoozing in the
corner, twitched an ear. Laura had taken Mrs White in with
her, to keep her company. Mrs White wasn't bothered.
She'd settled down on a piece of old carpet, given herself a
good licking and dozed off. The air inside the shed was hot
and suffocating. Laura sighed. Her shirt was sticking to her.
Her nose and throat itched with the dry smell of compost.

What if they go without me? she thought in sudden
panic. No – they wouldn't, would they?

She looked at her watch. One hour twenty-eight
minutes. One hour twenty-eight boring minutes she'd
been waiting to be found.

She was locked in the shed. She had locked herself in. It
was her final act of protest. Natalie had come up with the
idea. First thing this morning she'd leant out of her bedroom
window next door and called across, 'Hey, Laura, I've just
had this brilliant idea! Know what I'd do if I was you?'

So, there she was. Doing it. One hour twenty-nine minutes now. Silently protesting inside this smelly old shed. But no one had noticed. And no one had come looking for her. It didn't seem such a brilliant idea any more. What good would it do anyway? she thought. The removal men must have almost finished loading the van by now. But she couldn't just give up, could she? Not after all this time. She'd feel stupid unlocking the door and strolling out. She turned to Mrs White.

'What do you think then, Mrs White? Stick with it? Or not?'

Mrs White's ear twitched twice.

'That's one twitch for "No" and two for "Yes", is it?'

Laura sighed again and drew a face in the dirt of the window with her finger. It came to a sudden halt on the eyebrow.

What if they've already gone? Without me? At that moment she heard footsteps coming down the path.

'About flipping time,' she breathed with relief. And quickly rearranged her expression to one of inconsolable despair.

Her father peered in at the window and rattled the door.

In tones of great suffering (Laura had been rehearsing), she wailed, 'I'm not going, Dad. Just leave me here – I don't mind. I'll stay with Natalie. She's going to ask her mum.'

'Don't tempt me, Laura,' her father muttered. He rattled the door again. 'Come on, Laura! Don't be silly. Unlock this door – *now*!' He peered at her through the window again and jabbed a finger towards the door. Laura folded her arms. She heard his footsteps retreat. Then the face of her brother Nick peered in.

'You've had it now,' he grinned. 'Dad's gone to get one of the removal men. They're going to break the lock.'

Laura leered back at him and crossed her eyes. Before she had time to dodge he'd aimed his camera at her. Click.

'Nice one, Laura. Thanks!'

'That was a sick joke – giving you a camera for your birthday!' she yelled after him.

Her father returned with Mr Kelly and his toolbag. It took only a few minutes to get the door open. He was very nice about it. He winked at her.

Her father said, 'Satisfied now? With all the trouble you've caused?'

Her mother said, 'As if we haven't got enough to do, Laura, without this!'

Her five-year-old sister, Sarah, said to her fluffy pink pig, 'Laura's very naughty, isn't she, Prudence?'

Nick grinned and nodded.

With all the dignity she could muster, Laura stepped out and said, 'You know you're ruining my life, don't you?'

'Not another word, Laura,' said her father wearily. 'Just – just – wait in the car.' He dismissed her with a flick of the hand.

'My last words I'm saving for Natalie,' Laura declared dramatically. 'I'm now going to say goodbye to her. For ever.' She turned on her heel and left.

She found Natalie slumped over her front gate, watching the men secure the back of the removal van.

'It didn't work then?' said Natalie.

*

After that, Laura didn't say another word. Not for nearly four hours. Not even when they stopped at the Happy Eater and her father said, 'Laura, until you speak, I'll take it you don't want anything to eat. OK?'

As they travelled, Mrs White wailed occasionally from her basket. Laura felt like joining in. She caught her mother looking at her in the visor mirror. She twitched a half smile at Laura. Laura looked away. Regretting, then immediately justifying, the bother she'd caused. She tugged a magazine from her bag and flicked to the picture story. Someone had drawn moustaches on all the faces. A Hitler one here. A droopy one there. A few luxurious curly ones. Not talking was going to be more difficult than she'd anticipated. She glared murderously at Nick. 'You are so infantile!' she wanted to yell. 'I can't believe you were eleven last month!' He grinned at her. She slouched in her seat and stared out of the window.

As they passed under a bridge, Laura caught a glimpse of her reflection in the car window. A round, frowning face with smooth short hair. She wasn't like Nick who had thick sandy hair. Or like Sarah who had long dark curls. She liked to think of her own hair as chestnut. It sounded more interesting than brown. She had freckles, which she hated. Which multiplied in the summer and seemed to join up. Nick said her head was one big hairy freckle.

'Are we nearly there yet, Daddy?' said Sarah for the seventh time.

'Not far now.'

8

'How old did you say it was – our new house?' Nick asked.

'About a hundred and sixty years, give or take.'

'Which room am I having then?'

'You can sort that out between you,' said their mother over her shoulder. 'There are three nice attic rooms. Have to share for a bit though, till we get them done up. The place has been empty for quite a while.'

'What?' Nick made a grimace of pain.

Sarah cried, 'Goody! It'll be like camping.'

Laura blinked slowly and sighed again. Nick caught her eye.

'Hey, this is brilliant, this is. Laura not talking. You wouldn't think it was possible, would you? Hope she keeps it up.'

Laura grabbed Sarah's *Peter Rabbit* cassette and threw it at him.

'Stop! Stop! You'll break it!' screamed Sarah.

'Just pack it in will you!' shouted their father

'I think we should have turned off there,' cried their mother, her head swivelling to read the sign.

'Damn!'

The car braked with a squeal.

'Are we nearly there yet, Daddy?' said Sarah.

Chapter Two

It is well established that animals and small children are particularly sensitive to a ghostly presence.

THE HANDBOOK OF HAUNTINGS

'We're here. Glory hallelujah,' said their father.

There was the crunch of gravel and the squeak of the handbrake.

'Just look at that will you?' he said to no one in particular. 'That's Bath stone for you. Just glows in the sunshine.'

Laura had to admit – to herself – that the house did seem to glow. Its rough stones were pale and creamy. She wanted to hate it. Seeing it for the first time, she hated that she didn't hate it. It was not what she'd expected. She'd been misled by the smudgy photo on the house details her mother had showed them when she'd told them they were moving. She'd refused to show any interest. Though later she'd had a sneaky look.

Hillview House, Storrington, it had said. Nineteenth-century double-fronted residence built of Bath stone. Magnificent views of the Stor Valley. In need of updating and restoration.

Laura waited for the others to get out of the car. Then

she followed them and looked around. The front garden was very overgrown. Cans, crisp bags and other litter had been tossed in over the low wall. There were a few bungalows and cottages scattered further along the other side of the road, all built of the same pale yellow-grey rough stone. Beyond them the rising sweep and dip of hills and fields and sky. We've been dumped in the middle of nowhere, Laura thought.

A sudden gust sent the gate swinging on its hinges and the crisp bags scuttling. It swirled past and round her. As if inspecting this new arrival.

Laura headed for the front door. She heard Nick shout, 'Ffwaw! What's that stink?' His voice echoed off the walls.

'Probably the cellar – it's a bit damp! But don't go down there yet – there's no light!' their father warned.

The hallway was gloomy. A bare light bulb dangled from a wire. The paintwork was brown. In places paper peeled off the walls. A slither of envelopes, leaflets and newspapers lay behind the front door. The floorboards were dusty, scattered with rubbish. A rush of air followed Laura in, disturbing the litter and sending the envelopes sliding. She noticed a door beneath the staircase and opened it. The reek of damp and something worse wafted from the dark space behind it. She slammed it shut. Ugh! The cellar! she thought. At the end of the hall was the kitchen where she found her mother and Sarah. It was a large room with a big window overlooking a garden at the back of the house. Despite the sunlight, it seemed dark with its vast cupboards and dingy paint and walls. The large old-fashioned sink had a slimy rag in it. The floor looked as if it might dirty the soles of your shoes if you walked on it. And there was a smell that reminded Laura of drains. A door led to a passage out to the garden.

Sarah was hugging her pig, her eyes slowly taking in her surroundings. Their mother was rooting inside a box of toilet rolls and cloths and cleaners. She tugged out Ocean Mist airspray and squirted generously.

'It's horrible, Mummy,' Sarah said. 'Prudence and me don't like it. Why didn't you tell us it was horrible?'

It's revolting, thought Laura. I hate it. 'I bet it's haunted,' she mumbled.

Her mother looked at her. 'Don't talk such nonsense, Laura.'

Laura bent down to Sarah. 'Listen, Sarah – in *The Wizard of Oz*, when Dorothy is trying to get back home, all she has to do is click the heels of her magic shoes together, like this. And say, 'There's no place like home,' and *whoosh*! – she's there. Let's give it a go. Hold my hand. Ready?'

She took Sarah's hand, clicked her heels and together they chanted, 'There's no place like home. There's no place like home.'

Their mother let out a heavy sigh. 'This *is* our home. And you're going to have to get used to it, Laura. It's been neglected, that's all. It'll be lovely when we've finished with it.'

'It didn't work,' said Sarah, banging her heels.

'Worse luck. Need magic trainers,' said Laura as their father walked in with Mrs White in her basket.

'Oh, so it speaks,' he said peering over his glasses at her.

Laura wandered out to the hallway. Nick leant over a banister and shouted down, 'It's excellent! Take a look at the attic rooms – there's spiders' webs that must be prehistoric.'

Laura didn't answer. She was still not talking to Nick. The bare wooden stairs echoed as she climbed.

'Hey – it's like one of those horror films...' Nick's voice floated down from somewhere distant. '...you know – when they play screechy violins to let you know something nasty is lurking. Then – just as its victim reaches the top of the stairs – they build up to a scream as it leaps out...'

'*Aaargh!*' shrieked Laura. She fell against the wall clutching her heart. Nick had pounced just as she reached the landing.

'You stupid idiot! Don't you know how dangerous that is! I could have died from a heart attack! Mum! Tell him, Mum!'

'No such luck,' said Nick, sliding down the banister.

Laura peered down the stairwell. Sarah stood solemnly looking up, clutching her pig. Laura suddenly felt sorry for Sarah. For weeks their mother had been collecting cuttings from magazines. Pictures of rooms entitled 'A Bedroom Fantasy in Blue' or 'The Bathroom of your Dreams'. She'd say things like, 'Sarah – how would you like this lovely Mrs Tiggywinkle frieze?' And Laura knew that Sarah believed that's how it would be.

She made her way up to the attic rooms. She peered in cautiously. Each had a square paned window set into a sloping ceiling. Curtains of cobwebs draped the corners and the glass. She imagined giant spiders watching from the folds. She detested spiders. 'Yuk!' she shuddered, and made her way down to the middle floor. If she stayed too long, she'd be imagining all sorts of things.

Laura took pride in her imagination. Once, when the class had been watching a video on Native American tribes, Mr Starling had said, 'Laura Logan, you have the most vivid imagination I have ever come across.' This was after she'd heard Denny Barlow snigger an unflattering comparison between herself and a buffalo. Mr Starling had caught her whacking Denny over the head with an atlas. Not wishing to share her reasons with the rest of the class, she'd had to think quickly.

'I thought I saw a killer bee land on his head, Mr Starling.'

She wasn't absolutely certain that Mr Starling's remark was intended as a compliment. None the less, it had pleased her immensely.

Laura met Sarah and her pig on the landing. Together they explored the rest of the house. On the middle floor, three shabby bedrooms, one with a hole in the ceiling, and a grim-looking bathroom. They wandered downstairs. Two large rooms on either side of the hall at the front of the house and then another room at the back of the house, across the hall from the kitchen. It was cold and gloomy.

Laura squinted into the dark interior. Light filtered weakly through a dense mass of leaves outside the window, forming a shady puddled pattern on the floor. 'It's so dark in here.' She flicked on the light. It only seemed to emphasise the room's heavy bleakness.

Sarah hadn't moved from the doorway. She stood staring straight ahead, arms round her pig.

'What's the matter? Sarah?'

'It's so sad,' Sarah said in a small voice.

'What is?'

'It makes me feel so sad.'

'Yeah, well – the whole house is sad if you ask me. Come on.'

'Oh, look,' pointed Sarah.

'What?'

'Someone's looking at us through the window.'

'Where? I can't see anyone – Nick, I bet. Trying to scare us.'

In the kitchen their mother was busy scrubbing out the sink, their father unpacking the kettle and the teabags. Nick strolled in with his box of stick insects.

'This is your new home, Arnie,' he told Arnold Schwarzenegger, his favourite. 'Hey, Dad,' he went on, 'the bog's ancient and the bath's got green slime...'

'And have you seen the sink? It's totally disgusting,' added Laura.

'And how are you s'posed to lock the door – there's no lock,' Nick complained.

'You have to put your leg out and keep it shut with your foot,' said Sarah. 'I have to do that at school sometimes.'

'You'd have to be wearing stilts,' said Nick. 'The door's miles away from the bog.'

'You'll just have to whistle,' said their father. 'Till I fix it.'

'I can't whistle,' said Sarah, blowing to demonstrate.

'You'll have to sing instead. Now, listen, you lot. Less of the grumbling, eh? A little more co-operation? I'm sure you'll all rise to the occasion. I don't start my new job for another three weeks, so your mum and me are going to be up to our eyes with getting the place straight. Oh – and the workmen start on Monday – don't get in their way.'

'I'm going to have a look at the back garden,' said Nick.

Sarah skipped behind him. Laura followed slowly. The garden had run wild. Climbers, straggling roses and bindweed scrambled over the walls at either side. Creepers dangled from wooden arches over what had once been a path. The grass was knee-high. At the bottom, an old greenhouse leant against the wall. There were several fruit trees and a large tree with low dipping branches. Nick was dangling from one of them.

'This is the garden, Prudence,' Sarah told her pig. 'More like a jungle, really.'

After hours of self-enforced silence, Laura could not refrain from giving a growl. 'Better watch out for lions, then.' She clawed her fingers and sniffed the air in Prudence's direction. 'Hey – don't I smell a little piggy? A fat juicy little piggy.' She bared her teeth and snarled. Sarah screamed and ran off, giggling. Laura roared after her. For several minutes she forgot to be miserable. She chased Sarah round to the front of the house – and pounced. 'Grrrr. Yum-yum! Prudence stew for dinner tonight.' She grabbed the pig in her teeth, shook it and growled again. Sarah let forth a series of long, piercing shrieks. Within seconds, their father came striding out of the front door.

17

'Laura! Good God! What will people think? First day here! It sounds as if a family of vandals have moved in!' He pointed, 'Go on – inside!'

'It wasn't me. We were only playing. She was enjoying it, weren't you, Sarah?'

'I've just about had all I can take of you for one day! Do something useful – give your mother a hand. The van will be here soon.'

As Laura lugged the vacuum cleaner upstairs she heard her father say, 'I'm sick of it. Why does she always have to be the centre of attention?'

Laura remembered the last time he'd said that. Only two weeks ago. After she had quite unintentionally glued a red rubber glove to her head. When he'd had to come to Casualty to fetch her and Natalie home. 'You think I did this on purpose, Dad?' she'd asked in astonishment. (They had already explained, with diagrams, to the receptionist and the nurse how they had been perfecting their chicken costumes for the end of term show. Was it their fault the glue had run?)

Through the open bedroom window Laura suddenly caught sight of Nick ambling down the front path. She saw him lean over the wall. He peered up the road and beckoned. A blond boy on a bike came into view. He free-wheeled over to Nick. She saw Nick's lips move. The boy laughed and said something. Nick looked round. He caught sight of Laura at the window and yelled, 'Tell Mum I'll be back later!' He jumped over the wall, climbed on to the back of the boy's bike and off they went. Laura watched incredulously. They'd not exchanged more than a few words. What could Nick have said to make the boy laugh? *And* invite him for a ride! How did he do that? Then Laura saw the removal van draw up and her father directing it in.

Laura vacuumed until her mouth tasted of dust. She slid down the banister to find a drink. Sarah was sitting on a cupboard top, sucking a packet of orange through a straw.

'I've got a new friend,' she said.

'What?' Laura stared. How come Nick and Sarah had both got friends already? And all she'd got was the Hoover?

'Her name's Sadie,' said Sarah.

Chapter Three

A strong sense of being watched is often an indication
of a presence.

THE HANDBOOK OF HAUNTINGS

'How did you meet her then? You haven't been out on the road have you, Sarah?'

Sarah shook her head. 'In the garden.'

'Our garden?'

Sarah took a bite of biscuit and nodded.

'What was she doing in our garden?'

'Sitting up the tree.'

'Cheek! I hope you told her to clear off.'

Laura peered out through the window. 'Where is she then?'

'Gone,' said Sarah.

Their mother poked her head round the door. 'Laura, can you put the kettle on and make some tea for the men? Oh, and we'll need some more milk. Pop along to the village, can you? And get some biscuits.'

Thanks a bunch, thought Laura. I get the kettle, the teapot and the shopping bag too.

Turn right at the gate, her mother had said. Past the Recruiting Sergeant pub on the left, right at St Luke's on the corner and you're in the High Street. She passed the post office, the King's Head, a fish and chip shop and crossed over to the Spar shop where she bought milk and biscuits. She called at the newsagent's on the way back and bought a magazine and a packet of Rolos. Then she scanned the post-office window. The mobile library called alternate Thursdays. Mrs Fear had lost a white cat that answered to the name of Alaska. Dog owners were requested not to let their dogs foul the footpaths. The Parish Council had blah, blah, blah...

This place should be called Boring-ton, not Storrington, thought Laura.

She noticed the phone box on the corner. Dad had said they wouldn't have the phone on for a few days yet. She'd ring Natalie later. They could be miserable together. That would make her feel better.

Two men were wrestling a mattress through the front door when she got back to the house. Laura went round to the back. Sarah was sitting cross-legged under an arch, pulling rose petals from a climber and stuffing them into a jam jar. 'I'm making scent,' she called. 'Sadie showed me.'

'Well next time tell her it's *our* garden now. And she has to ask, right?'

'You're a bossy boots, you're a bossy boots, you're a bossy boots!' sang Sarah.

'Laura!'

Someone was knocking on a window. Laura turned. It was her mother beckoning urgently from the kitchen.

'Hurry up! What took you so long? Quick! Give me the milk, then go and call the men.'

As Laura reached the door, she asked, 'By the way – where's Nick?'

'I don't know. Just went off with someone. Ages ago.'

'With who?'

'Don't ask me. Some crazy-looking weirdo with a hand grenade. Only kidding.'

She took her magazine and her Rolos and went searching in the garden for some peace. She met Sarah going into the house with her jar of petals.

'You were rude to Sadie. You ought to learn some manners, she said. She doesn't like you.'

'Ha! She comes in without asking – and *I* need to learn some manners? Give me a break. Hiding was she? That's really sneaky! Where's she now, then?' Laura squinted down the garden.

'She's gone again. But she heard everything you said.' Sarah skipped into the house.

Laura hid herself behind the tree. She helped herself to a Rolo and flicked to the 'Share It' problem page of her magazine to see if they'd answered her letter. They hadn't. She had sent it eleven weeks ago. And a stamped self-addressed envelope.

Dear Share It
My parents have just told us we are moving. Just
when I got the part as the Wicked Witch of the West
in The Wizard of Oz *for next term. I don't want*
to go. But they just won't listen. We are moving 120
miles away. My best friend is very upset too. We have
been friends since we were babies. I cry myself to

sleep every night worrying about it. What can I do?
Distraught, age 12.

Distraught was Natalie's idea. She'd read it in one of her mother's magazines.

Laura had checked the post every day and the magazine every week. They had answered 'Help – I can't stop picking my nose', from 'A Distressed Person age 12'. Also 'Worried's' letter about 'My terrible fat legs'. And others. All whose problems were, in Laura's opinion, of much less urgency and importance. So Natalie had answered it for her.

Dear Distraught age 12,
This is totaly unfair. Do your parents realise how unhappy you are? Make sure you let them know.
A nice kid like you ought to be appreshiated more.
Your friend sounds like a very nice person.It beats me how they could do this to you both. You could try running away, but thats a bit risky. Cheer up. I will write to them personelly and tell them what I think.

Meanwhile I am sending you £100 for Letter of the Week.

There had been a hundred-pound note in the envelope. Drawn and coloured in painstaking detail. Instead of the Queen's head there was a photocopied school snap of Natalie. She was wearing a crown.

The sun disappeared behind a cloud. Laura heard someone call her name. She counted to a hundred. Then

24

another. She left the tree and wandered back to the house. Prudence Pig was lying face down on the grass. Above her fat pink legs, spelt out in large letters made of rose petals, was the word '*Sadie*'. A sudden breeze lifted them. They scattered and slowly drifted across the grass.

The van had left. One of the downstairs rooms was now crammed with furniture, boxes and stacked packing cases. The kitchen furniture was in place, looking slightly unsure of itself in its unfamiliar and grubby setting. Tea chests stood on the floor waiting to be unpacked. Several had been started, with balls of paper discarded on the floor. Nick strolled in the front door, bringing with him the smell of grass and windy fresh air, just as their mother called from upstairs. They found her in the big back bedroom. Their three beds and bedroom furniture had all been squeezed in. Nick's giant pinboard was leaning against the wall, covered with his photos: Mrs White throwing up in the flower bed with a speech bubble saying, 'Don't ever make me eat rat again'. Their father flapping up the beach in snorkel and flippers saying, 'I am a visitor to Planet Earth. I come in peace.'

Several weeks ago Laura had torn up the one of herself labelled, 'Great white whale beached at Southend'. She knew that her cross-eyed face leering through the shed window would take its place there eventually. With a stupid caption.

'Come on. You can help make up the beds,' said their mother, hauling bedding out from one of the big boxes. 'Then you can start unpacking what you need into the cupboards.'

Nick shuffled his feet impatiently, jingling the coins in his pockets.

'Where's Dad?' he blurted out the second she'd finished speaking.

'Under the sink doing something disgusting with a bucket,' said Laura.

Nick dashed out and ran down. They heard him call, 'Hey, Dad! Can we set up my computer – I want to show Shane.'

The reply from beneath the sink was explosive and brief.

Nick returned, shrugging as if to say, 'I only asked a simple question'.

Later, Mr Logan fetched fish and chips from the village, forgetting that Sarah hated fish and that Laura never ate anything that 'has walked, flown, hopped, wriggled, scuttled, squirmed or swum.'

'It could've just doggy paddled,' said Nick.

The smell of fish encouraged Mrs White to poke her nose out from her packing case. She had requisitioned it as a sanctuary from unfamiliar noises, smells and feet. She sniffed. Then, adopting an accusing look for the indignity of four hours' incarceration in a travelling basket, she retreated.

When their mother asked where Nick had been all afternoon, and who with and where did this boy live? Nick shrugged and said, 'Out and about. With Shane. I dunno.'

Laura knew that shrug. It was the one that said, 'Been nowhere, done nothing'. It meant the opposite.

'And it seems that Sarah's made a new friend, haven't you?' said Mrs Logan.

Sarah nodded smugly.

'Apparently she came into the garden to play,' their mother added with a meaningful look at Mr Logan.

'Really? I didn't see her,' he said.

'Nor me. She must have wandered in without us noticing. I don't think I want to encourage that sort of thing.'

'No, we don't. Or we'll have all the local kids wandering in when they feel like it,' said Mr Logan.

'One of the children from those new houses at the back, I expect,' Mrs Logan went on. 'Our fence backs on to their gardens, doesn't it? There's probably a gap and she's getting through.'

'Sadie says it's her garden,' said Sarah. 'She says it used to be lovely. And now it's a dreadful mess. She says you ought to do something about it. Quick sharp.'

'Did she, now?' said Mr Logan. 'Well, next time she wants to play, tell her to ring the bell and ask, will you, please?'

'See – told you – didn't I?' said Laura.

As their mother cleared the table, Nick slipped out to the garden.

'Give a hand with the washing up, Laura,' said her mother.

'That's not fair! I've done loads of jobs – Nick just skives off. Why can't he do it?'

'He always makes such a mess of it, then I have to do it all over again.'

'Stop whingeing Laura. Just do what your mother asks,' said her father.

Laura was almost speechless. Almost.

'He does it on purpose, Mum! That's his trick! He does it badly so you don't ask him again! Go on, Mum! Just make him do it and see.'

'You know, I think she's right,' said their mother. 'Nick!' she called from the back door. 'Come here!'

Nick hunched over the sink, dabbled feebly at the water with the brush. Unaware that he was being observed, he dropped a handful of cutlery on to the drainer. Then he hooked out a piece of soggy fish skin and carefully trailed it over them. Mr Logan roared with laughter. Laura didn't. Not until her mother made Nick start all over again.

'Hey, Nat! It's me!' Laura held five twenty pence pieces ready to feed into the slot when the pips went.

Natalie said she'd seen the new girl in the garden of Laura's old house and waved to her, but she'd ignored her. She was bored rigid already and didn't know how she was going to get through the holidays. She had bought a new pair of sunglasses that made her look mysterious.

Laura told her that the most exciting thing about Storrington was that the Spar stayed open till eight on Fridays. She described the house in horror-vision. Natalie said '*Ugh*!' in sympathy several times and said she would write a—

The pips went. Laura had run out of coins.

When she got back, two things happened. First she met

Nick running down the stairs with his camera.

'Oi – you know that terrible smell?' he said.

'The one in the kitchen?'

'No, the other one. You'll never guess what it is.'

'Your trainers.'

'A dead rat. In the cellar. You ought to see it. Maggots and stuff. It's gruesome.' He ran to the cellar door.

Then she heard her mother call from upstairs, 'Laura – have you seen Prudence? We can't find her anywhere.'

'She was on the grass!'

'Go and have a search will you, love?'

Laura went out to look. 'Prudence was definitely here,' she told Sarah. 'You must have moved her and forgotten.'

'I didn't. I left her doing some sunbathing. I just came back to show her my scent.' Sarah was clasping the jar of petals which were now floating in water.

Laura was tempted to say that perhaps the lions had got her, but, on seeing Sarah's face, decided against it. 'All right – let's have a pig hunt. Prudence!' she yelled.

Sarah looked round expectantly as if Prudence might come trotting out of the shrubbery. They searched in the grass and under the bushes. They peered behind the greenhouse. Wondering whether Sarah's new friend might have something to do with it, Laura explored the back fence. It was covered in brambles. The only gap was a tiny knothole. She squinted through and saw a small neat garden with a child's swing. As she turned, her eye was caught by something pink and furry. 'Look – there she is! Who put her up there, then?' Prudence was straddling a low branch of the big tree. Laura climbed up and tossed her down. 'I bet Sadie's been in again – she's got a nerve. Wait till I see her.'

Sarah hugged her pig then smacked her for going off.

'Sarah! Bedtime!' Mrs Logan called from the back door.

Laura watched her sister run towards the house, then followed. She saw Mrs White peek out of the back door, sniff several times and take a few cautious steps on to the pavings. The cat sat down again, sniffed the paving stones, looked around, then rubbed herself against Laura's legs. After further thought, she advanced with cautious steps to the grass. She suddenly stopped and stared, as if she could see something she didn't like. Her ears pricked up. She stared hard. Her body stiffened. The fur on her neck rose. Her back arched. She hissed. A look of pure astonishment passed over her face. Still staring, she backed off. Then she turned and hurtled back to the house.

Laura stood frowning down at the garden. What was all that about? she asked herself. Is Sadie here – hiding? Slowly, Laura retraced her steps. She searched behind the trees and under the shrubs. She looked in the greenhouse and up the tree. Walking back to the house, she noticed that the overgrown bushes covering the back room window almost completely obscured the space between the house and the garden wall. Pushing the branches aside Laura peered in and saw a dark passageway. She forced herself through. As her eyes adapted to the shade, she saw she was standing on a brick-paved path leading to the front of the house. Halfway along, she was surprised to see three steps jutting out from the house wall, as if there had been a door to the back room once and it had been filled in. The dark, enclosed space bothered her. She hurried on, pushing through a tangle of overgrown creepers and stepped out into the front garden. She made her way round to the back again, where she stood, arms folded, staring at the empty garden. 'Daft cat,' she muttered. 'Frightened of shadows.'

Quite suddenly she had a sense of being watched. Laura froze. Her eyes scanned the garden again. I know you're there, she thought. But where? With faked indifference, she strolled back to the house. The feeling of being watched intensified. Her spine began to tingle. She spun round. No one. 'Come out, come out, wherever you are,' sang her head. The long low branch of the tree bounced lightly. Just as if someone was sitting on it.

'Sadie?' she called softly.

There was no answer.

Chapter Four

It is common to dismiss children's invisible friends as mere imagination.

THE HANDBOOK OF HAUNTINGS

She would never admit it but Laura was relieved to be sharing a room that night. Despite his annoying habits, the presence of Nick sprawling on the bed across the room offered reassurance in this gloomy house.

There were no curtains at the windows yet. The sky was darkening. The window glass eerily reflected the room and its dim light bulb dangling from the stained ceiling. If she stared long enough at the stains, they took on hideous shapes; longer and they started to writhe and move. Laura blinked them away. Beside the sleeping Sarah, her pig was also staring at the ceiling; with small beady eyes. Laura was surprised and a little embarrassed by the comfort she got from a stuffed toy pig.

Nick was propped on his pillows playing with Sarah's *Etch-a-sketch*. 'Dad says he's going to fix the cellar up,' he said without looking up. 'So I can use it as a darkroom. Then I'll be able to develop and print my own photographs. I'm saving up, so don't buy me anything for Christmas. Or my birthday. Just give me the money, OK?'

Laura pointed out that this was August. And *his* birthday wasn't till next July. Anyway, he'd better not forget it was her birthday next. In two weeks' time. So he ought to be saving up for that. She'd be giving them a list soon. And he had to be joking if he thought for one millisecond she was going to give *him* any of her money.

'Just giving you plenty of notice. Think ahead. That's my motto.'

'If you think I'm going to *pay* you to make stupid embarrassing photos of people, you must be stark raving right round the twirly twist,' she said.

'Dad doesn't think so. Dad says I'm mature. He says I've shown a very mature attitude about moving house. Unlike some people not so very far away from where I'm lying right now.'

'Mature? Mature?' Laura screeched. She sat up in disbelief. 'Are we talking about the person who wanted to play the Longest Dribble of Spit Contest at my last birthday party? When he wasn't even invited? Are we talking about the person who stood in the queue in McDonald's with trails of Sarah's green Play Doh running out of his nostrils?'

'The very same. That was for a bet. I collected one pound and sixty-three pee for that one. Turn the light off. I'm knackered. You're the nearest.'

'Get lost! You were the last in.'

Laura turned her back to him. There were long runny stains on the wall. As if something wet had run down it. Blood, said her imagination. She shut her eyes. For a long time she lay there, her thoughts travelling back over

34

the day. Then back to the day their parents had told them they were going to move. She'd run straight round to Natalie's.

'Somerset? Where's that?' Natalie had said.

'Don't ask me.'

Nick had grumbled at first. About changing schools and missing his next judo grading. But after a few days, much to Laura's irritation, he'd shrugged it off. Sarah had chattered endlessly about the new Jemima Puddleduck cover and curtains she'd been promised for her new room.

'It's not the end of the world, Laura,' their mother had said repeatedly.

So, with Natalie's assistance, Laura had constructed a giant time chart counting off the days to 'Doomsday'. This was today. Moving day. She'd illustrated it with a diagram of the world exploding and labelled it 'Laura's World'. But Nick had changed it to a face with pimples and crossed eyes, broken teeth and a bald head sprouting three hairs. He'd crossed out the word 'world' and written in 'boyfriend'.

Nick's snoring brought Laura back to the present. The light was still on. She tugged the cover over her head.

'Well, what do you think of the house then, Laura?' said her father next morning.

Laura had her head in a cupboard looking for something for breakfast. 'I suppose it could be worse,' she said. 'There could be giant bats flitting around with blood dripping from their fangs.' She found the cornflakes and searched for a bowl.

'I hope Sadie comes to play,' said Sarah. She was in her

nightie, trying to balance Prudence on her head as she peered through the window into the garden.

'Tell me if she comes, Sarah,' said Mrs Logan.

'Who still sucks her thumb, then?' Nick teased Laura as he grabbed the cornflakes.

'What are you going on about,' said Laura who was trying to read, 'What Sort of Friend Are You?' in her magazine.

'You. You suck your thumb. When you're sleeping. Like a big baby.'

'I do not!'

'Oh yes you do. Caught you early this morning. On camera.'

He picked it up from the table and waved it at her.

'You're sick. Sick Nick. They gave you the right name all right. Quite pathetic really what gives some people pleasure.'

Still looking pleased with himself, Nick went off to take photos of the spiders' webs in the attics until their father suggested that he take some shots of the whole house as a record of it before the builders started work. Nick went out to the garden to get a long-distance shot. A short while later a faint cry for help was heard. Everyone rushed out. Nick was up the tree, caught by his shorts on a spiky branch, clinging upside down, unable to move forwards or back. The camera swung from his neck and he insisted on lowering that first. After a good deal of tricky manoeuvring, his father finally got him down, by which time Laura, unobserved during the rescue, had managed to take a number of interesting photos. She was particularly pleased with the one of Nick's bottom, when, for a split second, his shorts had got tugged down. Think ahead, that's my motto, she smiled.

'That's funny, thought I had more frames left than that,' said Nick, examining his camera.

Laura returned to her magazine.

Your best friend has had a terrible haircut. Do you:
a) laugh and tell her to go into hiding for a few
weeks, b) lie and say—

'Do I smell nice?' It was Sarah, dressed in her leotard and wellingtons. She was holding her jam jar and dabbing its soupy brown water on to her neck.

'For a frog, yeah!'

'Don't you like it?'

'It's intoxicating. Now go away.'

'Don't you want some then?' Daddy did. He rubbed it behind his ears. He said it would probably keep the flies away.'

'Attract them more like.'

Their mother came into the kitchen. 'Why are you dressed like that, Sarah?'

Sarah stared down at her boots. 'These are so I don't get prickled by the prickles in the grass. I got very prickled yesterday. And this is so I can do handstands,' she added, stroking her leotard. She wandered into the garden.

You tell your friend a secret, then discover everyone
knows. Do you: a)—

'Laura...'

Laura sighed. Her mother stood to the side of the window looking out. Without taking her eyes away from the window, she beckoned Laura over. '...come and take a look at this.'

Laura heaved herself up and looked. Sarah was sitting on the steps that led from the paved terrace on to the grass. She was chattering animatedly. To no one. She nodded. She appeared to listen. She leant forward and dabbed some of her scent on to empty space. She pointed at her wellies and waggled them. She jumped up, patted her leotard and did a demonstration of handstands.

'Well – that explains everything,' said their mother. 'No wonder we never saw Sadie. She's an imaginary friend. Mystery solved. Rather sweet really.' She watched, hands in pockets, smiling.

'I'm going to listen,' said Laura.

'Now don't go upsetting her. And no teasing.'

Laura stood inside the back door, straining to hear. She was too far away. She stepped outside. She heard Sarah say, '...curtains with Jemima Puddleduck and...'

Sarah stopped and looked round. 'Go away, Laura.'

'I'm not doing anything.'

Sarah grinned. 'Sadie says you should mind your own business.' She folded her arms and waited for Laura to go.

So, who put Prudence up the tree? wondered Laura. Nick, I bet. But what about all that other stuff? Mrs White scooting off – and that funny feeling there was someone there. That wasn't imagination, was it?

'Nick! Laura! Come on, make yourselves useful!' called their father. They found him in the hall.

'You can make a start on this wallpaper. I want it all off,

OK? Soak it well first, like this...' He demonstrated with a dripping sponge from a bucket of water.

Laura and Nick quite enjoyed it, for a while: splashing wet sponges at the wall – and at each other, scraping with the metal scrapers, peeling back long wet strips which they frequently flung at one another, while Laura told Nick about Sarah's imaginary Sadie.

'Well, it's an improvement on a fluffy toy pig,' he said.

Sarah appeared and said she wanted a scraper too.

Nick said, 'There isn't one. Where's Sadie then? Disappeared into thin air has she?'

'She's gone to look for her mummy and daddy. And Gus.'

'Who's Gus?' asked Laura.

'I don't know. I want a scraper.'

Laura tried to interest her in wetting the wall instead.

'Look – dunk the sponge, then splodge it on like this, see? You'll like this.'

But after a few attempts Sarah grumbled that her boots were full of water now and it was all their fault and stomped off complaining that they wouldn't let her help. Mrs Logan brought Sarah back with a box of crayons and said that for a very special treat she could draw on the walls where the paper was still on.

'Keep an eye on her, you two,' she added as she picked a cobweb from her shirt. 'We're cleaning the attics – it's filthy up there.'

'I'm going to draw me. And then I'm going to draw Sadie,' Sarah said.

'This should be interesting,' Nick muttered.

The doorbell rang just as their father came down the stairs with two bulging bin bags.

'I 'spect that's Sadie. I told her to ring the bell next time,' Sarah said.

Laura and Nick stared with interest as their father opened the door.

'How yer doin', Mr Logan?' said a cheerful sing-song voice. 'Nick in? I'm Shane.'

It was the boy with blond hair. He stepped in, his smooth flat hair shining like a helmet. He gave a brisk wave to Nick who had dropped his scraper and was wiping his hands on his T-shirt.

Shane beamed at Mr Logan. 'My dad says anyone who takes on this place needs all the 'elp he can get – and if yer need a carpet fitter, he's yer man. Also ligh' removals, 'edge trimmin', fancy pavin's and car valetin'.' His head bobbed in time to the words.

Mr Logan looked slightly startled. 'Well, thank you,' he said. 'I'll bear it in mind.'

'Ready?' said Nick, impatient to get away.

'Okey-dokes. That's a very nice car yer got there, Mr Logan,' called Shane, waving a hand at it as he walked down the path.

'Which one is Sadie?' asked Laura, turning back to the wallpaper and studying Sarah's drawing.

'That one, silly.'

Sadie had a very large head with what appeared to be a snake stuck to each ear. She had no neck, twigs for fingers and matchstick legs. There were balloons where her feet should have been. Sarah gazed at it admiringly. Then, with great care, she made two adjustments, adding a thick horizontal line to each balloon foot. Now they looked like shopping baskets.

'Those are her shoes. They're really nice. They're shiny black and they've got straps. Oh! I've forgotten to put the buttons on. And she's got a really pretty dress. It's blue.'

'Why has she got *snakes* on her ears, Sarah?'

'They're not snakes! They're her plaits.'

She added two bows.

'How do you spell 'Sadie'?' she asked.

Laura was draped over her bedroom window ledge in an attitude of boredom. It was Sunday. The sound of church bells mingled with the purring of lawnmowers and the sound of children's voices from the gardens beyond the fence. She went downstairs and yelled up, 'I'm going for a walk!'

No one answered. She searched the kitchen for a piece of paper and found her mother's shopping list. Someone, Laura knew who, had added: 'Mars Bars, cream slices, crisps, *not* cheese and onion, choc eclares, trifle, choc ripple ice cream'. Laura turned it over and wrote: 'Gone for a walk.'

She was picking out a selection of flying saucers, gobstoppers and other sweets in the newsagent's when two girls came in. They were about her own age. She watched them go over to the ice-cream cabinet and rummage around, discussing the merits of each item. She wandered over and peered in, hoping to think of something to say to them. Something to make them laugh and invite her round. She was still thinking when they left the shop, sucking on their Fabs.

Laura walked around for a bit. Up the main road, past an old steep-roofed school, right to the estate of new houses and a small park with swings. Apart from people mowing their lawns, washing their cars or walking their dogs, nothing much seemed to be going on. She found some money in her pocket and tried phoning Natalie, but there was no answer.

When she got back, Nick was still out. Her parents were doing things to the kitchen. Her mother attacking the paint with a sander, her father prising strips of something off the floor. The hallway was piled with things from the kitchen, including Nick's stick insects. She found Sarah and Mrs White asleep on the sofa in front of the television. A lady in a tiara was singing earnestly to a man in a top hat. Laura flopped down into the armchair and, sucking on a gobstopper, watched the man in the hat take the lady into his arms and tap dance across the screen.

'I'm back!' Nick's shout woke Laura up. The television roared as racing cars skidded round a track. Sarah had gone. She heard Nick talking to his insects. 'What you been doing all day, Arnie?'

'Dinner!' called Mrs Logan.

Dinner turned out to be tinned potatoes, hardboiled eggs, cheese, squashy tomatoes and some leftover cake.

'What – no roast potatoes?' said Nick.

Sarah came skipping in from the garden, looked at the table, fetched a knife, fork and plate and set out another place next to her own.

'This is Sadie's place now. Here you are, Sadie – you can sit down here.'

Nick rolled his eyes at Laura.

'Oh – she's in the house now is she? This I can't wait to see.'

'She's been in before, you know,' said Sarah with a secret smile.

When their father came in and nearly sat on the chair next to Sarah, she screamed, 'Careful, Daddy! You nearly sat on Sadie!'

'Very sorry, Sadie,' he smiled at the empty chair.

'I don't believe this,' muttered Nick.

Laura couldn't believe it either. She couldn't believe it when Sarah put a potato, a slice of cheese, half a boiled egg and a tomato on the plate. Or, seconds later, when she noticed that her own plate had a tomato and the one on Sadie's had disappeared.

'Who put that there?' she demanded. 'I don't want it – it's soggy.'

'Sadie,' said Sarah. 'She doesn't want it either. She says she hates tomatoes.'

Laura noticed that both her parents found this very amusing.

'How old is this Sadie, then?' said Nick.

'How old are you, Sadie?' Sarah asked the chair. 'Seven and three quarters,' she told Nick.

'So how come she's invisible?' asked Laura.

'She's not invisible, silly. She's real. It's just that you can't see her. She says only very clever, very special people can see her.'

Their father laughed out loud. Their mother, leaning on her elbows, smiled fondly at Sarah. 'Would Sadie like some cake?' she asked.

Nick nearly choked.

'Yes, please. With lots of icing.'

Their father laughed even louder.

'Your uncle Howard used to have an imaginary pet rabbit,' said their mother. 'It was called Dobby. He carried it around in his pocket. It escaped once and we all had to pretend to search for it.'

Their father said, 'I read somewhere that imaginary friends are usually a sign of high intelligence. It certainly shows remarkable imagination.'

'Mr Starling said I have a vivid imagination,' Laura told them.

'Pass the salt,' said Nick.

'It's wasting food, putting it out for someone who isn't there,' said Laura.

'She can have my potatoes,' said Nick. 'They're disgusting – they taste of tin.' He leant over and scraped them on to Sadie's plate. Laura decided to add her egg to it.

'She can have this too. Yuk. Look at all those green bits.'

Sarah scowled at them both. 'Sadie says you are the most perfectly dreadful children she's ever met.'

Mr and Mrs Logan laughed.

'I think she may be perfectly right,' nodded their father.

'Sadie can go take a running jump,' Laura said.

'Ugh!' Nick spat out a mouthful of tea. 'And she can take you with her, Laura! What d'you do that for?'

'Do what?' said Laura.

'Put salt in my tea!'

'I never!'

'Liar!'

'Shut up the pair of you!' ordered Mr Logan.

Laura poked at her food with her fork and glared at Nick. He ignored her. A small potato suddenly flew across the table, bounced off Nick's head and landed on the cheese.

'Oi! Cut it out will you!' he yelled.

Sarah, her hands over her mouth, shook with laughter.

'Right! That's it, Laura! I won't have you playing with food!' cried her mother.

'What? That's not fair! I haven't done anything!'

Her father's knife and fork clattered on to his plate. 'Laura, is it too much to have one day without—'

Laura stood up, scraping her chair noisily. Mrs Logan held up her hand like a traffic policeman. 'Let's calm down, shall we? Laura, just apologise to Nick and we'll forget all about it. All right?'

'But I didn't *do* anything! Why pick on me?'

'I wonder,' said her father.

Laura stared at him. 'It wasn't me!'

She turned and marched out. She ran down to the phone box and dialled Natalie's number again. Still no answer. She found a seat in a bus shelter and sat there, her head swirling every accusation and injustice into a frenzy. Anger gave way to self-pity. She'd show them. She could easily catch the bus into Bath. Then take the train to... But how much would that cost? At the last count she had £7.92 – less the Rolos and her magazine would leave... Not enough anyway.

*

Who *did* throw the potato, then? thought Laura as she lay in bed that night. Nick couldn't have thrown it at himself. It certainly wasn't Dad. Or Mum. Could it have been Sarah? And what about Prudence up the tree? And 'Sadie' written in petals? Sarah didn't even know how to spell it, did she? And there was that funny feeling of being watched in the garden. Mrs White knew something too. Something very odd was happening in this house. And whoever, whatever Sadie was, she seemed to be at the centre of it.

It was dark now. Laura could barely make out Nick's bed. The chair against the wall slowly took on the shape of a crouching figure. She squeezed her eyes shut. But things like that don't happen, do they? she asked herself. Not without a sensible explanation. Do they?

Chapter Five

Most ghosts haunt a particular place.
Usually the place where they lived. Or died.
THE HANDBOOK OF HAUNTINGS

Laura's thoughts were briefly diverted by the arrival next morning of a letter from Natalie.

Dear Distraught age 12,
Are you bored? Fed up? Try this amazing FREE
Anti-Boredom Kit.

Inside there was another envelope. On the outside Natalie had printed:

Have fun making your own jigsaw puzzle.

Laura opened it. There was an old Christmas card with a picture of a robin on it, and a sheet of paper. It said:

Instructions
1. Carefully cut picture from back of card.
2. Draw jigsaw shapes on to picture.
3. Cut out shapes.

4. Have fun putting it back together again to make a beautiful picture of a robin.

There were a few jokes. A drawing of herself in her new sunglasses. A Garfield sticker saying 'Are we having fun yet?' And a fingernail wrapped in tissue which said,

This was my best fingernail till it broke. WRITE BACK. I am so bored.

The house was now busy with men pulling up floorboards, carrying rolls of wire and long shiny pipes and hacking at walls with chisels. There wasn't a room in the house without some noisy, smelly or dusty activity. Nick had taken his football and gone off with Shane again. Laura took herself out to the garden to write a letter back to Natalie. She settled under the tree. Mrs White snoozed under a bush near by.

Dear Bored Person age 13,
Why not have a go at this simple quiz. Just arrange the first leters of each answer to make a well known word.
1. Small furry thing with wings that goes buzz buzz and makes honey.
2. The number that comes before two.
3. A colour. Begins with R. Three letters.
4. Big lumpy grey thing with a trunk.
5. You have to do this before—

Laura jumped as Mrs White suddenly leapt from under her bush. But she was only chasing a butterfly. It fluttered out of reach. Mrs White pretended that she hadn't really been trying and didn't care anyway. She flopped down beneath the tree and licked her leg.

Seriously, Nat. Some weird things have been happening here. Sarah keeps talking about a friend she calls Sadie. Mum and Dad thinks it's an imaginery friend and how it's really cute. It's sick making. And Mrs White keeps acting strange. Like she can see something, only there's nothing there. I think it's...

Laura sucked her pen. She wasn't sure what she thought. When she read it through it seemed silly. She added,

a ghost. Something odd is going on here.

It seemed even sillier. She tried again. After half an hour she'd added a doodle of a small face with plaits, and the word 'Sadie' printed and shaded to look three-dimensional. She threw down her pen. She wasn't in the mood for writing letters. She looked up to see Sarah trying to pedal her bike through the long grass. She was wearing her nurse's outfit. 'I hate this grass,' she said. 'It's wearing my legs out.'

Laura clasped her foot and fell backwards. 'Nurse – quick! You're just in time! I've been bitten by a poisonous snake.'

'Goody-goody!' said Sarah, abandoning her bike. She tucked Prudence under her arm and tugged out her first-aid case from the basket. And while Sarah did things with her toy stethoscope, syringe and little mirror-on-a-stick-thing, Laura asked her about Sadie.

'Is Sadie bigger than you, Sarah?'

'Yes.'

'Does she talk to you?'

'Sometimes. Mostly we play.'

'What does she talk about?'

'About you and—'

'What about me? Never mind looking in my ears, I've got flipping snake bite, not earache.'

'I told you – keep still! I'm trying to look.'

'What did she say about *me*, Sarah?'

'Mmmm. Bossy. Rude. And very nosey. Open your mouth, please.' Sarah poked her toy thermometer into Laura's mouth. 'And she saw you take Nick's camera.'

'What!' Laura spat out the thermometer. 'She didn't.'

'She did. She said you were clicking the button thingy.'

Laura looked at her little sister. How could she know that?

'You're making it up. *You* saw me using his camera, didn't you. Sarah?'

'Nope.' said Sarah, peering at her thermometer. 'Two hundred and nine,' she said, shaking it. She put it back in her box. 'You've got to have an injection now.'

She *must* have seen me, thought Laura.

'You mustn't tell Nick about the camera. It's a surprise, right? Photos of him being brave.'

Laura glanced round the garden. 'Is Sadie here now, Sarah?'

Sarah shook her head. She didn't know why Sadie hadn't come today. But Sadie knew all sorts of interesting things. Like how to make scent. And her six times table. And how to spell rhinoceros. Sometimes she was suddenly there, and suddenly not there. Just like that.

The confident, knowing way in which Sarah chatted about Sadie disturbed Laura.

'Maybe she's a ghost,' joked Laura. 'Can you sort of see through her?'

'Don't be silly,' said Sarah. 'She's real.'

'Only to you. No one else can see her, can they?'

'They're not special like me.'

'Hey, Sarah. Tell me the truth. Was it Sadie who threw the potato?'

Sarah gave a guilty smile and nodded. Her response made Laura even more uncomfortable. She wanted to be reassured that Sadie *was* just imagination. That there was an explanation for everything. If you looked hard enough.

'Why didn't you say something, then?' she said at last. 'You should have stuck up for me.'

'I was going to. But then she said it was a secret. She did this.' Sarah pursed her lips and pressed a finger to them.

Laura stared at Sarah. 'Was Sarah really clever enough to be making all this up?'

'She must be a ghost,' Laura said half to herself. 'If she was real we'd all be able to see her, wouldn't we?'

Sarah gave a long sigh that said she *knew* Sadie was real and that's all there was to it.

'Why is she here then, Sarah?'

'I told you – it's her house.'

'Where does—'

'You're giving me a headache,' sighed Sarah. 'There. All better now.' She patted Laura's knee. There was a Winnie the Pooh plaster on it.

Laura watched Sarah pedal off. 'She's making it all up,' she told herself. 'It's only Sarah's pretend game.'

The rest of the day passed slowly. Laura began almost wishing for signs of Sadie to pass the time. She found the robin Christmas card and drew jigsaw shapes over it.

After the workmen had finished for the day, their mother told them to freshen up and change. They were going out to eat. When Laura came downstairs she found Sarah chatting away to Sadie on the sofa. Mrs White was nowhere to be seen.

'That? Oh, that. That's a television,' Sarah told the armchair. 'It makes pictures. Look – see?'

'Ready, everyone?' called their father, jangling his car keys. 'Switch the telly off, Sarah.'

'But Sadie's watching it, Daddy.'

They drove into Bath. They strolled past the Roman baths. They stared up at the abbey with its angels climbing ladders to heaven. They crossed Pulteney Bridge then gazed down at the River Avon as its water gushed over the weir. They stared in the shop windows offering postcards and souvenirs. They peered at the grand houses and buildings. Their father admired the flowerbeds and the hanging baskets. Their mother told them about the hot water which bubbled up from natural hot springs deep in the ground and which filled the famous baths that had given the city its name. How the Romans had built a city here. And, ever since, people had come to bathe in and drink the water as a cure for illness. Sometime during the holiday, she promised, they could visit the baths and taste the water.

'When are we going to eat?' yawned Nick.

It was three against two for pizza.

When they got back, Mrs White was scratching at the back door to be let in. She poked her head round, scanned the room, sniffed and stepped in.

'Silly girl,' said Mrs Logan, 'Where have you been?'

'Where's her food, Mum?' said Laura.

She fetched a tin from the cupboard and forked it into a bowl. As she returned the tin to the shelf she noticed marks on the grubby back of the cupboard door. She squinted at it and rubbed with her finger.

'Hey! What's this? There's writing or something.'

Nick went over. 'It's a height chart isn't it?'

'So it is,' said their father, peering over his glasses. 'What's it say?'

Laura knew what it said. She'd been staring at it for several seconds. 'You're never going to believe this. Look at these names. One says Sadie. The other says Gus.' Her stomach fluttered. She could taste her pizza. She thought she heard violins screeching. It was true. Everything that Sarah had said was true.

'Ah-ha,' said their father. 'So *that's* where Sarah got the name from. She must have seen it here on the door.'

'Of course,' said their mother, smiling at Sarah. 'Clever

Sarah! Fancy spotting that.' She went over and peered at the door. 'Look, doesn't this say nineteen twenty something? How interesting.'

Laura looked at them with disbelief. 'No way, Dad! Sarah couldn't have seen this.'

'We ought to keep that – gives a bit of history to the house,' said her father, wandering over to the tap and filling the kettle. 'Who wants a cup of tea?'

'Yes, please,' said Mrs Logan. 'You're right – we ought to leave it. I saw a notice in the post-office window – there's going to be a photographic exhibition of old Storrington in the village hall. Must remember to pop in and take a look.' She sat down and reached for the paint colour charts on the table. 'You know, I'm still not sure about this blue,' she said. 'What do you think?'

Laura stared at them all. Nick was communicating silently with Arnold Schwarzenegger. Sarah was trying to plait her hair.

'You know what I think,' announced Laura. 'I think that Sadie died – and that this house is haunted by her. That's how Sarah knows about her – because she can see her. But she's the only one who can see her and... '

Her father turned slowly, the kettle in his hand. 'Of course, Laura. Now why didn't I think of that? And no doubt she's come to help us find the long-lost buried treasure.' He smiled at his own joke.

Nick gave Laura a sad look.

'Mr Starling was right about you, Laura,' said her mother. 'You certainly have a vivid imagination.'

Laura looked desperately at Nick. 'But Sarah even knew

about Gus! Come on, Nick! You remember! The other day?'

'Yeah – but it was all on the door, wasn't it? She saw it. It's obvious.'

'Sarah. Did you see this on the door?' Laura demanded.

'Yes – there it is. It says Sadie. I told you she was real.'

'Not just now, Sarah. Did you see it before – before Sadie was your friend? Come on, Sarah!'

Sarah yawned. Laura flapped her arms in frustration. 'Anyway, she can hardly read yet!'

'I *can* read. I'm on Yellow Book Two,' said Sarah.

'OK then, Sarah. Tell Mum and Dad what you told me. About Sadie. How she used to live here. And how she talks to you.'

Nick snorted. Mr and Mrs Logan exchanged a look. Sarah screwed up her face and looked up at the ceiling.

'She used to live here, her name's Sadie, she talks to me – and she's my friend.'

Mr and Mrs Logan laughed.

'And it was Sadie who threw the potato too. Go on Sarah – tell them.'

Sarah sucked in her cheeks.

'That's enough, Laura,' said her mother. 'You're going too far – as usual. Do you want some tea or not?'

Laura looked at them looking at her. She knew what they were thinking.

After Sarah had gone to bed, Mrs Logan said, 'Laura, are you deliberately trying to frighten Sarah? All that talk about hauntings right in front of her, just before bedtime? Really – I sometimes wonder whether you ever think at all.'

'Haven't we had enough silly games over the last few

weeks?' added her father. He put an arm round her. 'Come on, love. You're nearly thirteen – only ten days now. Time to grow up a bit, eh?'

Later that evening, when no one was about, Laura found a cloth and rubbed away some of the grime from the door. The wood hadn't been painted. Pencil lines showed different heights up the door. Names and dates and ages had been written alongside in a sloping, curly handwriting. The lowest one read:

Gus – third birthday, 7.3.15.

Both Sadie and Gus had been measured at regular intervals against the door, recorded with dates and ages. Laura squinted at the door, trying to decipher the figures. She worked her way up to,

Sadie - seventh birthday, 12.1.23.

Sadie had measured three foot nine inches. Higher up, she read,

Gus – eleventh birthday, 7.3.23,

and marked at four foot eleven inches. There were no more entries after that.

Chapter Six

The paranormal: occurrences, abilities and phenomena
which cannot be explained by science.

THE HANDBOOK OF HAUNTINGS

I bet Sadie died. That's why the chart suddenly stopped. I wonder how? It must have been a bit later – Sarah said Sadie was seven and three quarters didn't she? She must have died about nine months after being measured. And what about Gus? What happened to him? Did he die too? Perhaps they were both in an accident or something. But I'm not going to think about them. Not till tomorrow.

Laura plumped her pillow. She turned over and tried to get comfortable. She turned this way, then that. She tried lying on her front. I wonder if Gus is dead? If he's alive he'd be...

After some concentrated adding and subtracting Laura came up with ninety-one. But then again he could be dead too. Sadie must be dead. That's why... *I am not going to think about it!*

Lying there in the dark still room, Laura's senses seemed to tune in to every tiny sound, every shadow. She could hear Nick's slow breathing. The whole house was sleeping. In daylight, Sadie was just an annoying, if invisible, visitor. In the dark she was the creak on the stair, the shadow in the corner, the shape at the end of the bed. Laura closed her eyes and tried to relax. Sadie and Gus, Sadie and Gus, repeated her head. Sadie and Gus!

'Gus! Gus!'

Someone was calling for Gus. Laura sat up with a jolt. At the end of her bed stood a little girl. A girl with a long black plaits, a blue dress and white bows. She laughed and tugged at the bed cover. Laura screamed. And woke up. The room was still and dark. The luminous digits on Nick's clock glowed 00.57 in red.

'Nick?' she whispered urgently. He didn't answer. The clock's red seven flipped into eight. She saw that her cover had slipped to the floor. She tugged it back up and burrowed under it. After much tossing and turning and telling herself the problem was an overactive imagination, caused by too much three-cheese pizza, Laura fell asleep.

Sarah got a ticking-off next morning when screws from the electrician's toolbox were found scattered on the floorboards of one of the attic rooms. Some of them had been arranged to form a large letter S.

'It wasn't me. It was Sadie,' she said.

'Well make sure she doesn't do it again,' said their mother.

'Huh?' said Laura loudly. 'What did you just say, Mum?'

'There's a big difference between make believe and fabrication, Laura,' she said.

'Why don't you tell Mum and Dad the truth, Sarah?'

said Laura later. 'You made me look a right idiot last night.'

'I did tell the truth. I said Sadie's real. But they don't believe me. And the potato is a secret. I promised. You can't keep secrets, you can't.'

'Not when it means I get the blame for things I didn't do.'

In the rare moments when there was no one in the kitchen, Laura kept returning to the cupboard door. Someone took a pencil and made those marks on the wood, she thought. Wrote in those names. More than eighty years ago. More than eighty years ago, seven-year-old Sadie stood against this door. And Gus too. She imagined them standing against the door. Sadie in her blue dress and black strapped shoes. And Gus in an old-fashioned collar and sturdy boots. Laura measured herself against it with the handle of a spoon. I'm taller than you, Gus. Who were you? What happened to you, eh?

Early that afternoon, Shane turned up again, head bobbing. 'How yer doin' then?'

He followed Nick into the kitchen to see his stick insects. Laura was sitting at the table adding up her score on 'What Sort of Friend Are You?'

'Now this one's Arnold Schwarzenegger – the boss. That one's King Kong – but he's useless. Lost two legs already. They shed them, see, if they get caught and want to escape. That one's Mrs Twiglet. Go on, see if you can find the others. It's hard to see them sometimes.

59

Perfect camouflage, see. How many do you reckon are in there, eh?'

Shane's head bobbed more than usual as he counted. 'Five.'

'Nine,' said Nick. 'What we going to do now then?'

'Mum said she wanted some shopping done,' said Laura from behind her magazine. 'Your turn. I did it yesterday.'

'That's only my sister – just ignore her.'

Shane bobbed and grinned.

'Stupid magazine.' Laura tossed it on to the table. She had scored six out of ten.

'It's not the magazine that's stupid,' said Nick. 'She thinks this house is haunted.'

'Yeah?' beamed Shane. 'My dad saw a ghost once. Riding an 'orse. On Fossdyke Road. Vanished before his eyes it did.'

Laura was beginning to prefer Shane to Nick.

Nick shrugged. A shrug that said 'Yeah, well *that* story's perfectly believable. But my sister's – that's stupid.'

'What's it look like, then – this ghost?' said Shane.

'She's a girl – with plaits. And shiny black shoes. She used to live in this house. Until 1923. Then she died. Aged seven and three quarters.'

'She's crazy,' said Nick.

'I am not. Ask Sarah. And look at the back of that door if you want proof.'

'Oh yeah – I believe Sarah,' mocked Nick. He turned to Shane. 'Sarah's my kid sister who has this imaginary friend called Sadie. After a name she saw written inside that door there? She also has a fluffy toy pig that she talks to. Und zis sister here ees a most interesting case. She keeps raving about zis ghost girl. A ghost zat throws potatoes! She ees quite, quite mad. Vot think you, Herr Doctor Shane?'

Dr Shane grinned and bobbed.

'Is your head on elastic or something?' said Laura.

'Now you see what I have to put up with,' said Nick.

'At least I don't talk to little green insects,' she said, doodling an S pattern round the edge of her magazine.

'Wouldn't catch my mum livin' in a place like this. She likes modern. She 'ates dirt,' said Shane.

'Who used to live here then?' said Laura.

'I dunno. Bin empty for ages. There might've bin an old bloke 'ere once – went into a home or something. Tried gettin' in once – no luck. Those apples trees are good uns though.'

Mrs Logan came looking for Sarah.

'She's watching telly. With Sadie,' Laura told her.

'Not again? I'll take her shopping with me – where's my list?'

But Sarah didn't want to go shopping. She refused to turn the television off, because Sadie was still watching it. But Mrs Logan switched it off and said in her 'let's-pretend' voice, 'Oh, I'm sure Sadie can find something more interesting to do while we're gone.'

Sarah kept telling everyone how much Sadie *loved* television. Her favourite programme was *Sesame Street*. She also had strong opinions, on everyone and everything, which Sarah passed on to everyone. Mr Logan's colourful shorts were funny. But Laura's made her bottom look big. Nick found this hilarious. 'Big Bum Logan,' he mocked.

Mrs Logan had nice hair. But it was a pity that Laura's was so mousy and straight and not like Sarah's which was very pretty. Nick, not home very much, escaped lightly with a remark on his talent for spitting.

'She likes Nick,' giggled Sarah. 'She thinks he's handsome.'

'Leave it out!' said Nick indignantly.

Their mother should get someone to do all the work. And use hand cream. And when was all this horrid noise going to stop?

When everyone was out, Laura asked Mr Lee, the electrician, if he knew anything about who'd lived in this house. But he lived in Radstock and didn't know. Then she had the idea that the previous owner, the old man, might be Gus. So she went out to the back and rummaged in the bin bags for the letters that had been lying in the hall when they'd arrived. They were covered in smelly cat food and other rubbish. She found one addressed to The Occupier. Then a card to Mr W. L. Robson reminding him his eyes had not been tested since February 1987. She tossed them back.

She wandered out to the front garden, leant over the wall and peered down the road, looking out for a girl on a bike that she could beckon over. A bus passed. Then three red cars in a row. A lady with a pushchair. A yellow dog trotting purposefully on stubby legs towards the pub.

On this perfectly normal summer's day, Laura began to

wonder whether she *was* being over-imaginative. She tried to convince herself she was. In which case, she thought, Sarah's imagination was amazing – inventing all that stuff about Sadie. I suppose Nick could have put Prudence up the tree. Not that he'd admit it. And I suppose Sarah might have seen the names on the door. Perhaps Sarah *is* clever enough to make up all this pretend stuff. And it's quite normal for cats to be *nervous* in strange houses, isn't it? But what about the flying potato? And the salt in Nick's tea?

No, she decided. Sadie was real. If a ghost could be real. And if she wasn't on the receiving end so much, it might even be funny. She liked to think that if she ever became a ghost, she'd quite enjoy that sort of game herself.

She wandered back towards the house. Mr Samson, the plumber, was sitting on the front step, pouring himself a mug of tea from his flask.

'You're missing *Neighbours*,' he said, waving his flask in the direction of the hall.

Laura heard the theme tune blaring out from the television. Someone had switched it back on. She peered in from the doorway. She imagined Sadie sitting there in her shiny shoes, stroking one of her snaky plaits, smugly pleased with herself. She felt a tiny shiver trickle down her back.

'It wasn't me. It was Sadie,' Laura said when her mother returned and asked why the television had been left on.

Her mother gave her a hard stare and a loaded sigh. It wasn't long, however, before Sarah's 'imaginary' Sadie and her fondness for television began to cause general nuisance. Next day, when Mrs Logan was vacuum cleaning, Sarah said, 'Mummy, can you do that later, please? Sadie can't hear what Big Bird is saying.' And she complained when their father popped in and flicked over to catch the news. 'Oh, Daddy – we hate the news.'

Mrs Logan asked if Sarah couldn't pretend that Sadie wanted to do something more interesting? Like having a nice picnic in the garden? But Sarah said that would only make Sadie sad, because she couldn't actually eat anything. Sarah usually insisted a place was set for her at the table, though, in case she turned up, and so she wouldn't feel left out. There was no doubt when she did, because Sarah would pass on all Sadie's opinions. She thought the house was 'a terrible mess', and wanted to know 'when will all this noise stop?' It was clear that both their parents found Sarah's chatter and inventive 'imagination' regarding Sadie all very entertaining. But most of the time they were too busy, and Nick not around enough, to notice how Sadie's influence on Sarah was growing. Laura, for whom time hung heavily, and who had nothing better to do than wander about looking for something to do, was the only one to notice that Sarah was clearly bored with television. One morning, Laura found her doing backbends on the sofa during *Sesame Street*.

'Fancy a game of Kerplunk?' Laura asked.

'OK.' But then Sarah sighed and said, 'Sadie says be quiet 'cos she can't hear the telly.'

'Well, tell her to mind her own flipping business. Come on – we'll play in the kitchen.'

Laura gathered up the sticks and the marbles. Sarah hesitated in the doorway and put on a 'shall I – shan't I' face. 'She doesn't want me to – you've upset her now.'

Laura threw down her sticks and demanded, 'OK! Where is Sadie right at this moment, Sarah?'

Sarah pointed at the armchair.

'Right, that's it!' Laura told the armchair. 'Are you listening, Sadie? We're playing – so tough if you don't like it. And if you think I'm bossy, then just take a good look at yourself!'

When she heard her own voice loudly giving the armchair a piece of her mind, Laura felt rather silly. It had to be the precise moment, too, that Nick came strolling in. He put the tip of his forefinger to the side of his head and made screwing movements with it, then backed out. Laura marched to the television and turned it off. As she plonked herself crossly on to the sofa, it switched itself back on. She stared, frowned, jumped up and switched it off again. Just as she sat down, it switched on. Again she switched it off and stood there ready. It clicked on and burst into noisy life. Laura jabbed it off. On, off. On, off. On, off. On, off. On, off. On... She gave up and ran out to the hall.

'Nick! Come here! Quick! Watch this,' she said, switching the television off again. She stood waiting for Sadie to switch it on.

'Well?' shrugged Nick. 'Watch what? I mean – wouldn't it be sensible to switch it on first?'

'No. Just watch, Nick,' Laura insisted.

He looked at her staring at the screen, slowly shaking his head, as if his sister had an incurable disease. 'I don't know which is more sad. Shouting at an armchair – or watching a blank screen. You are seriously strange, Laura. You need help. You are off this planet!'

'It was switching on by itself! Honest, Nick. Every time I switched it off, it came back on again. I'm not kidding – ask Sarah!'

Sarah sat on the sofa, an innocent smile on her face.

'Tell him, Sarah! It's not funny!'

'You're right there,' said Nick. 'Not funny ha-ha. It's funny peculiar.'

He left. Sarah fell back, laughing.

'Shut up, Sarah.'

'I can't help it – she's poking her tongue out at you.'

Laura poked out her tongue at the armchair.

'She's not there,' giggled Sarah. 'She's next to the telly.'

The television switched on. Then off, on, off, on, off, on. And stayed on. Laura stood stiffly, hands clenched. Well – I know for certain now. You are not imagination. And I know you don't like me. Because *I* won't play your games like Sarah. But you're not going to tell *me* what to do, Sadie What-ever-your-name-is. She thought it with more bravado than she felt. She glared in the direction of the television, then ran upstairs and threw herself on to her bed.

Help, she thought. What do I do now? It's all right for Sarah. Mum and Dad think it's clever and funny because Sadie is only a game. A make-believe friend. Nick thinks she's a joke. But if *I* mention Sadie, then I'm going too far, aren't I? Or, according to Nick, going mental. She *is* the ghost of Sadie. The one on the door. You see stuff like this on the telly, but you never really believe it do you?

Laura remembered a programme about haunted houses. They'd sent in a psychic investigator. Disembodied, that was the word she'd used. When someone dies, the investigator said, their spirit leaves their body and off it goes to the spirit world. But sometimes it doesn't. Sometimes it gets stuck. Sometimes they don't even know they are dead so they hang around. It looked as if Sadie had got stuck. Or maybe the spirit world had sent Sadie back. She wouldn't blame them. Probably got fed up with her, thought Laura.

She started to imagine herself as a lost spirit. She'd come back and haunt Nick. That would teach him. But what if no one saw you? There you were, trying to tell Mum and Dad you were there. But they couldn't see you or hear you? No wonder you heard stories about things being thrown around. You'd have to, wouldn't you? To get some attention. Or worse, what if you came back and everyone you knew had gone? Died even. And you were all alone? Well – you'd be dead pleased to find someone who could see you and hear you and be a sort of friend, wouldn't you? A friend like Sarah. And you'd probably want her all to yourself and get a bit jealous. And you wouldn't be exactly pleased to find strangers living in your house, would you? She rolled over and sat on the edge of the bed.

What am I doing? Why am I feeling sorry for Sadie? All the trouble she's caused me. And she's really crafty. Got everyone thinking Sarah's sweet. Got Sarah doing what she tells her. Keeping secrets. And always chooses just the right moment to play her tricks. Behaves herself in front of

Mum and Dad. Unless she can put the blame on me. Like the flying potato. But she can't scare me.

Oh yes she can, said a small voice in her head.

Laura looked at her fingernails. She'd bitten them right down.

By the end of the week, Sadie had became a sort of family game. They could pretend that Sadie was there. They could laugh and nod and talk to her as if she was. But when Nick accused Laura of hiding his trainers (he found them under Laura's pillow), and she protested her innocence, pointing out that she'd rather pick up a cow pat with her bare hands than his trainers, and that it was probably Sadie, she saw a look of irritation cross her father's face. However, she decided to try just once more to tell her mother what was going on. She practised in front of the wardrobe mirror. She would explain calmly. She anticipated her mother's expression. Changing from disbelief to uncertainty, to horror, to apology.

Laura went to find her. She was in the kitchen, standing on a chair, measuring the window. 'Mum – what if...'

'A hundred and forty-seven centimetres,' said her mother. 'Write it down on that pad there will you, Laura?'

Laura wrote it down and tried again.

'Mum – what if – if Sarah doesn't really want to watch telly all that much? And what if there *were* such things as gh—'

The tape measure made a zipping sound as it whizzed back into its black plastic case. Her mother turned towards her. 'And what if we just put an end to all these ridiculous ghost stories,' she sighed.

68

'But she doesn't even *like* telly very much.'

'I'm warning you, Laura, this is getting very, very boring. And now you mention television, don't I remember some programme about such nonsense? Is that where all this comes from?'

'But, Mum, loads of people have seen ghosts – or heard them. It can't all be nonsense, can it?'

Her mother considered Laura for several seconds. She climbed down from the chair. 'Look, love, believe me – there are no such things as ghosts. Here or anywhere else. You shouldn't believe everything you see on telly, you know. They're just stories. Some people enjoy that sort of thing – they like the thrill of being frightened – like the ghost train at the fair. They're for entertainment. But we all know it's not true. And despite all the stories of ghosts, no one ever has been able to prove a single one exists.' She gave Laura a squeeze.

'Trouble is you've got far too much time on your hands at the moment. Look – things'll get better, I promise. How about Natalie coming for a few days, once we're sorted? How does that sound?'

Laura stared down at her feet and gave a tiny nod.

'Now stand by that side of the window and hold the end of the tape for me, will you?'

Yet, later, when their mother found that all the biscuits had been eaten and that the empty bottle in the fridge was all that remained of the milk, Nick grinned, 'Don't look at me. P'raps it was Sadie.' And when their father mislaid his screwdriver, he could be heard muttering, 'Right, Sadie, what have you done with it, eh?'

*

The telephone had been connected. A shiny red phone hung from the kitchen wall. Laura was impatient to ring Natalie. She waited till their mother was putting Sarah to bed and their father had gone to finish some paint stripping in the bathroom. She dialled Natalie's number, just as Nick came in with some privet leaves for his insects. Laura replaced the phone noisily.

'Do you have to do that now! I'm trying to phone!'

'Don't mind me.'

'But I do mind – shove off, Nick.'

He ambled over to the cage, searched for Arnold and carried him to the table on his finger.

'Hurry up, Nick!'

'Arnold needs a bit of exercise. How would you like to be in a cage all day? Huh?'

Then he added, 'Though from the way you've been acting lately, that's where I reckon you ought to be.'

'Why don't you just let them go then? They'd be much happier, wouldn't they? Insect brain!'

Eventually Nick wandered off and Laura tried again.

'Hi, Nat! It's me! We've got a phone. Want to take the number?'

'Hey – you owe me two letters,' said Natalie.

'What? I sent one – definitely. I put it on Mum's pile for posting. And I rang you on Sunday...'

'Sunday? Oh yeah – I was out.'

'Do anything interesting?'

'Swimming.'

'Swimming? Who with?'

'Shelley.'

'Shelley! Not Shelley Prentice? But we can't stand Shelley Prentice!'

'She's not that bad. Anyway it's better than doing nothing. It's worse for me – left behind. At least you can meet new people.'

'No I can't. There's no one round here. Not till I start school. And I'm dreading that. I hate it here, Nat. There's absolutely nothing to do.'

She could hear Natalie breathing and *EastEnders* on the television in the background.

'Hey Nat – don't laugh, but I think this house might have a ghost.' It came out in a rush.

'Yeah? Wow! What's been happening?'

'Well, first Sarah's toy pig went missing – and then this potato flew across the room and—'

Natalie screeched with laughter. 'You're crazy,' she said eventually. 'Oh yeah – did I tell you? The new girl next door's called Tara. And I'm thinking of having my hair cut...'

But Laura had stopped listening. She wasn't alone. An uncomfortable sensation was crawling up her back. Someone was behind her. She spun round. The kitchen was empty. 'Nat! Nat!' she called into the mouthpiece. Her eyes darted round the room. But the line was dead.

She slammed the phone back on its hook. It missed, and swung wildly. Laura saw something rise slowly from the table. A stem of privet leaves that Nick had left. It hovered in mid-air. Suspended by an invisible hand. It started to sway from side to side, then swooped towards her. She staggered back against the wall as it brushed her face then fluttered to the floor. A tea towel lifted from the draining board and started to flap towards her like a huge, blind bird. She dashed for the door, slamming it behind her. She dived across the hall to the sitting room. Nick, watching a programme about hippos, looked up with an expression of annoyance. Shutting the door firmly behind her, Laura took a deep breath and with relief dropped on to the sofa next to him.

'Watch out! Talk about hippos!' he complained.

Laura waited for her heart to slow down. She glanced at Nick, bursting to tell him. I've got to make *someone* believe me, she thought.

The hippo programme finished but Laura didn't notice. She was aware of a crash somewhere. And someone shouting for Nick. She saw Nick get up and go and heard more shouting. Then Nick was storming back in and yelling at her.

'What?' she blinked.

'You killed him!' He was yelling at her. 'You – you – *murderer*!'

Chapter Seven

Some spirits, particularly those of children, seem to take a mischievous pleasure in the effect they have on the living.

THE HANDBOOK OF HAUNTINGS

'She murdered Arnold Schwarzenegger! It must have been her! She was the only one in here, wasn't she? And you ought to have seen her when she barged in. Talk about looking guilty! Anyway – who else could it have...'

'That's not fair! I was nowhere near...'

'Shut up! The pair of you!' shouted their father. 'Right! Your version first, Laura.'

Laura explained that she'd been nowhere near his stupid insects. She decided it was not a good moment to give her opinion that this was all Sadie's doing.

Then Nick told his version. 'She said I ought to let them go – that's proof isn't it!'

Mr Logan closed his eyes and massaged the bridge of his nose. Apparently, Mrs Logan had walked into the kitchen a short while ago to find the cage's lid off, several insects roaming free and Arnold dangling from Mrs White's mouth. She had tried to rescue him but Mrs White had dashed out to the garden, where Arnold had been crunched and swallowed before her eyes. The cage was now minus the murdered Arnold and three other insects.

'And who was it who left the phone off the hook?' said Mrs Logan.

'Laura, of course,' said Nick. 'She was phoning Natalie, wasn't she? I told you she was in the kitchen.'

'Well?' demanded Mr Logan.

'It was an accident – I didn't mean to!' she blustered.

'You didn't mean to? It was just an accident, eh?' said her father. 'Perhaps you didn't mean to lift the lid off the insect cage either? Was that just an *accident*, too, Laura?' he asked with exasperation.

'Yes! I mean – no! I hate them, Dad! I didn't go *near* them! Do you really think I'd do a thing like that?'

He looked at her in a way that clearly said he did. Nick leaning against the wall, scowled at Laura. 'I do,' he muttered.

Laura turned and rushed to the door. She wouldn't let Nick have the satisfaction of seeing her watering eyes. The phone rang. Mr Logan reached for the receiver. 'Oh – hello, Natalie – yes, yes – she's here...' With a look that said, 'Be quick', he held the receiver out to Laura.

'What happened? The line went dead. I've been trying to get through for ages,' said Natalie.

'Er, I don't know. It just cut out...'

Nick continued to glower at her. Her father tapped his fingers on the table, her mother folded her arms and waited.

'Look – I can't talk right now,' Laura muttered, turning her back on them. 'It's not a good time. Yeah – speak to you later.'

'If you didn't do it, then who did? Answer me that,' Nick demanded the second she'd finished. 'Sadie was it?' he scoffed. 'Sadie the ghost?' He screwed up his face and wriggled his hands towards her, like a cartoon spook.

'Don't let's get started on that again!' said their father.

Laura stood stiffly, blinking at them. 'Right then – blame me! If it makes you all feel better! May as well – I get the blame for most things round here!' she cried, turning to go.

'OK, OK, love. That's enough,' said her mother putting her arm round Laura. Laura stared at the floor and bit her lip hard.

'If you say you didn't, then there's no more to be said.' Mrs Logan turned to Nick. 'It's quite possible, Nick, that Mrs White could have knocked the lid off. She's been out all day – hasn't been fed yet. And she's been very tetchy lately. Also – it's quite possible that you, Nick, didn't shut it properly. It's happened before, remember? When we found Bilbo Baggins in the Frosties?'

Nick gave a shrug that said, 'Yeah, but I still think Laura did it.'

'If it makes you feel any better,' his mother added, 'it was very quick. I don't think Arnold suffered at all. And he was getting on a bit. Quite an old age pensioner, as stick insects go.'

'No one deserves to be chewed to death. He should have had a decent burial at least,' said Nick.

Mrs White walked in, looking pleased with herself. She gave the kitchen a thorough looking over, padded to her empty bowl, turned and miaowed loudly.

'That cat is behaving very oddly these days,' said their mother. 'Never budged from the sofa at one time. Now we hardly see her.'

'She's had her starters, now she wants her main course,' said Mr Logan. 'It's all this country air.'

No it's not. It's Sadie, thought Laura. Are you here? Smiling at all the trouble you've caused? Knowing that I can't do anything about it.

'What was all that noise about?' Sarah stood in the doorway, one hand trailing Prudence, the other rubbing her eyes.

Going to bed in a creepy house is bad enough, thought Laura as she brushed her teeth. Going to bed knowing Sadie might be creeping about is double creepy. Going to bed knowing she might be creeping about – only you can't tell anyone because they think you're making it up – is triple creepy. She'd left the door ajar, and kept glancing over her shoulder as she brushed. The bare bulb cast thick shadows in the gloomy bathroom.

'What's she going to do next?' Laura asked her reflection in the pitted mirror over the basin. The shadows reflected in the glass seemed to distort. She gave an involuntary shudder, threw down her toothbrush and hurried out.

It's so weird, she thought as she undressed. The way Sarah behaves like it's perfectly normal to have a friend no one else can see. She doesn't think Sadie's creepy, does she? And why does Sadie keep picking on me? What have I done? What if she turns up in the dark, she thought.

76

Or when I'm asleep? Or perhaps she only comes when Sarah's awake. Hey, maybe it's something to do with Sarah *wishing* her here. She hasn't shown up at night. Or has she? What about the other night? Did I dream that or what?

'Sarah?' Laura said as she got into bed. 'Did you see Sadie after you came up to bed?' She concentrated on sounding calm.

Sarah shook her head.

'Has she ever come into this room at night?'

'Don't think so.'

'Don't you think it's just a bit weird that you're the only one who can see her, then?'

Sarah was lying on her back, twisting a thick strand of hair into a corkscrew. 'No. I told you – only special people can see her. Most people don't even know she's there. They can't see her. She waited ages and ages for a friend. She got very lonely. She waited for Gus too. Waited and waited. She got fed up of waiting. So she went to look. Then she got lost. Then she came home. But she couldn't find anyone. Not Gus. Or her mummy or her daddy. She was very sad. But she's happy now. 'Cos she's got me.'

'What happened to them all?' asked Laura sitting up.

'I don't know,' said Sarah. 'I wish I had plaits,' she yawned.

'It was Sadie who let Nick's insects out, you know, not me,' Laura told Sarah. 'She came in when I was there. Couldn't see her, but she was definitely there. She was trying to wind me up – moving things and sending the tea-towel flapping at me. Then, when I'd gone, she let Arnold

Schwarzenegger out of his cage – and I got all the blame. I'm fed up with her. Just tell her to stop annoying me, will you?'

'It's her house, you know. It's only playing.'

'What else did she tell you, Sarah?'

'I can't remember. Stop talking.'

Nick came in later. He tugged off his socks and trainers, then his jeans, and climbed into bed.

'You're disgusting,' said Laura. 'Aren't you going to wash? And your trainers stink! Put them outside or something. I can't breathe!'

Nick put on his Walkman headphones and turned his back to her. Laura could hear its tinny beat. She wondered if smelly trainers might have the effect of keeping ghosts away, like garlic was supposed to keep away vampires. I hope so, she thought.

'He never washes,' said a sleepy voice. 'When Mummy said to wash his knees when we went out for pizzas he only pretended – he just put talcum powder on them. *And* he left the seat up.'

Sleep was impossible for Laura. Not for Nick, spreadeagled on his back, mouth open, headphones askew, or for Sarah, sprawled upside down on top of her cover. Laura burrowed her head under her duvet. Her head was a tangle of thoughts. The more she tried to unknot them, the more tangled they became. Her head ached. I couldn't even get Natalie to believe me, could I? I mucked that up all right. She thought I was kidding. She doesn't seem to miss me much, does she? I mean – Shelley Prentice! And she's made friends with Tara next door. Don't think about it. Don't think about Sadie. Don't think about any of it. Think about something else. What do I want for my birthday...

She heard her father climb the stairs. The landing light went off. The room was plunged into blackness. Every nerve in her body seemed to tingle, as if all her senses were on alert. The lights of a passing car sent shadows rippling across the walls. Laura shut her eyes. Somewhere a pipe gurgled. She let out an exhausted sigh, turned over and wriggled down. Go away, Sadie, she breathed. Go away, go away...

'I don't want to go away. I want to come too.'

Laura is in a garden, hurrying along a path. Velvet green lawns either side, flowerbeds spilling colour. Through an archway cut into a tall hedge. Neat rows of lettuce and vegetables, a shed, a greenhouse.

'You can't.'

'I'll tell.'

Turning round. Sadie stands there, hands on hips, defiant. One plait flung over her shoulder. Wearing a yellow dress and bows. White stockings and shoes. Beyond her, the house.

This is only a dream, Laura told herself, in her sleep. My head is full of Sadie. She won't go away. Now I'm dreaming about her.

'Tell what?'

'That you took some of Daddy's cigarettes. I saw you.'

'Sneak.'

'Pleeeese, Gus. Let me come. I'll be good.'

'Not now – another time. But only if you don't sneak.'

I'm not me, Laura told herself, as in her dream she reaches a gate in a wall. I'm Gus. I'm dreaming about Gus now. And this is our house and garden. Only it looks different. Through the gate, into a lane. No new houses. A row of what looks like stables. Running along the lane. Ahead a grassy slope now. Climbing up. Reaching the top of an embankment. A railway track stretching to the left and right. Striding off to the right, parallel to the track. A long way off, the glimpse of a black chimney, and a tower topped by a large wheel. The wind carrying a choking smell. A sharp taste on the air that sticks in the throat. There is a distant chunky clanking sound of metal. Off to the right now, down the bank, half skidding, half sliding. A glimpse of booted feet and thick socks. Heading for a clump of trees. Inside – a sort of den, roofed by foliage of overhanging branches. A mossy floor. Kneeling down. From a pocket withdrawing a paper bundle. Peeling back the paper. Two large buns. Two apples. Four sweets in twists of coloured paper. A small tin. Glimpsing inside, two cigarettes and a folder of matches. Laying them out on the mossy ground. Sitting and waiting.

Laura opened her eyes. In that split second of wakening, she was confused. Where am I? Where's my old room gone? she thought. Bright sunlight streamed into the room through the curtains. Then she remembered. She leant up on her elbow and squinted towards Sarah. No Sarah. Or her bed. Everything was different. Where they should have been, a large polished wardrobe stood against the wall. She rubbed her eyes and looked again. Sarah lay sleeping, her arms flung above her head. Opposite, Nick slept face down, a foot hanging over the edge of his bed. Laura lay back. Did I imagine that, dream it, or what? she asked herself.

Chapter Eight

*Some people who have experienced a haunting choose
to keep it to themselves, for fear of ridicule.*
THE HANDBOOK OF HAUNTINGS

Laura was last down for breakfast next morning. She stared at Sarah eating her Rice Crispies. Her hair had been arranged in two thick plaits. Their mother was opening the post.

'Looks like another letter from Natalie,' she said tossing an envelope over.

'Who did her plaits?' said Laura.

'Sadie,' said Sarah.

Laura blinked and gave her mother a hard look that said, 'Right Mum, explain that. If Sadie doesn't exist how come she's given Laura a new hairstyle?'

'I showed her how to do them yesterday. Clever, isn't she? Did them all by herself.'

Laura bit back what she wanted to say. She picked up her letter. On the back it said, *Write back or else!*

'Mum?' she asked. 'Did you post my letter to Nat the other day. I left it on your pile. She said she never got it.'

Her mother frowned. 'I don't remember seeing it or posting it, but perhaps I just didn't notice it.'

'Spoken to any ghosts lately, then?' grinned Nick, looking up from his comic.

'Laura says it was Sadie who let Nick's insects out,' said Sarah with a mouthful of crispies, then repeated everything Laura had told her. As Sarah babbled on, Mrs Logan fixed Laura with a stare. Her nostrils flared slightly. Nick shook his head as if to say, 'You are one sad case, Laura.'

Mrs Logan began to clear the table noisily. 'Oh look, Sarah. Daddy's left his tape measure,' she said, picking it up. 'Be a good girl and take it up to him, will you?'

Sarah skipped out. Nick leant on his arms, watching Laura with a smug smile.

'Haven't you got anything better to do, Nick?' said their mother.

'I was just waiting to hear...'

'Go!' she ordered.

Laura picked up her letter and turned to go too.

'Not you, Laura.'

Laura stared down at the letter.

'Look at me, Laura.'

Laura sighed and flicked her a sideways look.

'This has got to stop, Laura. All these nonsense Sadie stories. No more. You understand?'

'It was only going along with Sarah's make-believe stuff,' said Laura.

'I want it to stop. You hear me?'

As Laura climbed the stairs she heard Sarah singing from inside the bathroom. She stood and listened with her ear to the door.

A sunbeam, a sunbeam, Jesus wants me for a sunbeam!
A sunbeam, a sunbeam! I'll be a sunbeam for him!

Where did she get *that* from? thought Laura. Checking that no one was about, she turned the handle and pushed the door slightly open. Sarah was at the far end, sitting on the lavatory, legs dangling .

'Where did you get that, Sarah? Was it Sadie?' she whispered.

Sarah screamed, 'Go away, Laura!'

The door slammed in Laura's face. She knew it couldn't have been Sarah.

'Serve you right, Nosey!' said Nick, as he ran past and slid down the banister.

'You're very quiet today,' said her father later. 'What's that mark on your face?'

He looked down at Laura from his stepladder.

'I walked into a door,' she said. 'Where's Mum?'

'Gone into Bath, taken Sarah with her.'

Laura leant against the doorframe and watched him run the paint roller down the wall. Natalie's letter had been mainly doodles and jokes. Then a P.S.

Been next door. They've got Sky TV – there are loadsa films. And they're going to get cable too. Tara's OK.

It left her feeling even more low and moody. She'd planned to ring Natalie tonight, but now she didn't feel like it.

It would only make her feel more out of things. She'd been lying on her bed, doing a lot of thinking. It hadn't got her very far. And she couldn't shake off her dream. She found herself constantly looking over her shoulder and jumping at noises. All the time wondering whether Sadie was there without her knowing it. Every small thing she said or did, Sadie could be watching. She'd report it back to Sarah. And later Sarah would announce before everyone, 'Laura was so bored she was playing with my Barbie doll. And she pinched seven of my Smarties. Then she was poking around in Nick's things for ages. She found his cash box and tried to get it open. She even tried on his Nike top. Then she went and made this *huge* peanut butter and jam sandwich. Then she had a Penguin. And *five* HobNobs. And if you want to know who finished off the Pepsi, well...'

'Here – you have a go if you like.'

Her father climbed down his ladder. 'Watch me – like this, see? I've got a spare roller – somewhere.'

'You've dropped a great dollop of paint, Dad.'

Slowly, the morning passed.

Mrs Logan and Sarah returned loaded with shopping bags. Sarah rushed upstairs and stood before her mother's mirror holding a Jemima Puddleduck pillowcase against her chest. Then she draped it over her head.

'Don't tell me you're planning to wear it,' said Laura from the doorway.

'I want to see what it looks like.'

'Listen, Sarah,' she said quietly, stepping in. 'Don't

repeat everything I tell you about Sadie, OK? You got me into trouble this morning.'

'But you told me...'

'Yeah, I know. Just keep it to yourself next time. It's all right for you to talk about her – they think it's just pretend – you're only five...'

'I'm nearly six.'

'Promise. It's just between you and me what I tell you. Promise.'

'All right,' Sarah sighed.

She turned back to the mirror and mimed sleeping on her pillow case, using her arms as a pillow. Then she went off to try them on her bed. Laura studied herself in the long mirror. She noticed a long drip of paint on her favourite T-shirt.

'That's all I need,' she told her reflection.

'Have you seen Prudence anywhere?' asked Sarah from the doorway.

'Why ask me?'

Laura wandered about aimlessly. She tried reading but reached the end of a page without knowing what she'd read. She flicked on the television and zapped from channel to channel without interest. She went back to the bedroom where her mother was fixing curtains at the window.

'There – only old ones. They'll have to do for now.'

Laura frowned. 'What about the other ones?'

'What other ones?'

'That were there last night.'

'Last night? You must have imagined them. Here – take the steps and put them on the landing.'

Laura came back into the room and stared at the window. They were part of my dream, weren't they? It's the same window. And there was that big wardrobe. What's happening to me? Can't even tell what's real and what isn't any more. It's this house – it's doing things to me. And Sarah. She caught sight of Sarah in the garden, kneeling on a blanket on the grass, wearing her nurse's outfit. So Prudence has turned up then. And Sadie too, if I'm not mistaken.

Laura pushed up the bottom of the window. Laura couldn't hear Sarah. A lot of drilling was going on in the room next door. But she could see her nodding and chattering as she wrapped a bandage around the pig's head. She watched her listen to Prudence's chest with her stethoscope. Sarah looked up, as if listening to someone. Then she knelt up, hands on hips and shook her head. She got up and dawdled towards the house. She hesitated, turned and looked back. Then she continued towards the house and disappeared from sight. Shortly afterwards, she reappeared. She had something in her hand. Something long and shiny. Laura leant forward and peered hard. It was the bread knife.

'Sarah! What are you doing?' she shouted.

Sarah turned and looked up at her, the knife glinting in the sun.

'Stay there!' Laura ordered and raced down.

Sarah stood still, looking over her shoulder towards the blanket.

'Give that to me, Sarah!' Laura called as she ran towards her.

'But Prudence has stopped breathing – we've got to do an operation on her.'

'Not with a real knife, Sarah!'

Sarah thought for a second then said, 'She's very ill. She's got dip-theer-ia. You can't breathe when you've got dip-theer-ia. You have to cut their throats. Here,' she said, pointing to her own throat. 'To let the air in.'

'Dip what? Anyway, you can't cut her with that! You'll rip her to bits! She won't be the same again you know – even if you sew her up.'

Sarah chewed her lip as if she wasn't all that happy herself with the idea of sawing through Prudence's neck with a large and very sharp knife. She frowned and glanced over her shoulder again.

'Sarah, is this Sadie's idea?'

Sarah swivelled her mouth from side to side.

'She's here, isn't she?'

Sarah stared at the grass and kicked it.

'Is this Sadie's idea, Sarah?'

'No,' she mumbled.

What's going on here? thought Laura. Instead of her usual chatter, Sadie says this and Sadie says that, she was pretending that Sadie wasn't even there. But Laura knew that Sadie *was* there. Watching.

'Give me the knife, Sarah.'

Sarah sighed heavily and handed it over. More a sigh of relief than annoyance, Laura thought.

'Mum would go mad if she knew you were playing with this. It's very sharp – you could have an accident – cut your finger off or something.'

Sarah looked at her fingers and blinked slowly. Laura decided to go along with the game.

'You could try the kiss of life on Prudence. You know, when you breathe into her mouth. That'd make her better.'

Sarah cheered up visibly and skipped over to her pig.

'Careful you don't blow her up, though.'

Sarah bent over Prudence, then stopped, looked up, turned and said, 'I can't do that, silly. I could get germs. You can die from germs, you know.' Then she laughed and added, 'You can go now, Miss Laura Nosey Parker.' She giggled into her hands, glancing sideways as if sharing the joke with someone.

Laura narrowed her eyes and targeted where she thought Sadie might be. She imagined her kneeling beside Sarah on the rug. Whispering into her ear, telling her what to do and what to say. Sulky and a little cross now because she wasn't getting her own way. Trying to get her own back at Laura for interfering. Getting round Sarah by making her laugh.

'No thanks – it's my garden too,' said Laura, sitting herself firmly on the steps. It appeared to Laura she'd scored a bull's eye. Sarah's eyes shuttled back and forth from Laura to the rug.

'I'm not playing that game any more.' She frowned and tugged at a tuft of grass. 'You spoil everything you do! Spoilsport! Spoilsport!'

'Right – come inside!' ordered Laura, leaping up.

'No!'

'Yes!' She grabbed Sarah's hand and dragged her to the house.

'Mum!' Laura called.

Sarah wriggled and shrieked, 'Let go of me! Leave me alone! Get off!'

'What on earth is going on down there?' Their father peered down at them over the banister as Laura dragged her protesting loudly up the stairs. Their mother was hurrying down now. 'Laura – for heaven's sake! What are you doing with that knife?' She took it from her and they followed her down to the kitchen. 'Now what's this all about?'

'I found Sarah playing with this, Mum! She was going to cut up Prudence pig!'

'I wasn't! I was going to do an operation! It was only playing.'

'But you mustn't play with knives, Sarah love,' said Mrs Logan, kneeling down. 'That was very silly – and very dangerous. You won't do it again, will you? Promise me?'

Sarah nodded.

'She was going to cut Prudence's throat...' said Laura. She took a deep breath. She must make them try and understand. 'And I don't think it was *her* idea,' she finished.

Her mother stood and slowly folded her arms in the way Laura knew meant serious business, and looking hard at her, said sharply, 'Really, Laura? Whose idea do you think it was, then?'

'Tell her, Sarah.'

Sarah scowled. 'Mine – I told you!'

Mrs Logan looked at Laura, her eyebrows arched like question marks. She didn't say, 'Haven't we had enough of this Sadie nonsense?' again. She didn't have to.

'OK,' Laura blustered, 'don't take any notice of me, but playing with knives is not *my* idea of a jolly little game for a five-year-old. Good job I was there – that's all I can say.'

'Yes, you're right,' sighed their mother, 'and I'm glad you took it off her. But you just can't stop at that, can you? You know what I'm talking about.' She rubbed her forehead as if she had a headache, then glanced down at Sarah. 'Look, Laura...' She pushed back her hair wearily. 'Never mind – we'll talk about it later.' She waved Laura away. 'I think we all need a break. There must be six layers of paper on those walls up there. Go and ask Mr Lee and Mr Samson if they want tea or coffee.'

Sarah was gone when Laura came back. Mrs Logan was putting biscuits on to a plate. Through the kitchen window Laura saw Sarah down the garden again, her back to the house, looking down at a flowerbed. She found her staring down at a little mound of soft earth sprinkled with daisies and rose petals. Sarah looked up at Laura and wailed, 'Prudence died! We had to bury her – and it's all your fault!'

'What!'

'That's what—' Sarah checked herself. ''Cos you wouldn't let me do the operation!'

'I don't believe this! Is that what Sadie told you? Well, serve you right. Why don't you listen to me instead of Sadie? I don't know why I should feel sorry for you! Not after the trouble you've caused me.'

Sarah sniffed.

'So whose idea was it to bury her then?' Laura sighed,

looking down at the little mound of earth. A little garden trowel, taken from the greenhouse, lay next to it.

Sarah wiped her nose, leaving a muddy smear. 'Mine,' she blinked.

'No, Sarah. It wasn't,' said Laura sharply. 'It was Sadie's, wasn't it?'

Sarah gave a tiny, sorry nod.

What game is Sadie playing now? thought Laura. She bent down. 'Look, Sarah, you mustn't let this – this girl boss you about. She's not nice. I suppose she's gone now has she? After causing all this trouble,' said Laura, feeling not a little envious of the means to vanish at awkward moments.

Sarah gave a grumpy pout.

'Don't worry – we'll just dig her up again.'

'She – I'm not s'posed to.'

'I don't believe this either,' flapped Laura. 'She's even got you doing what she wants when she's not around. Left you instructions has she? Come on.'

'We sang "All Things Bright and Beautiful" at the funeral,' Sarah said as Laura tugged the pig out.

'It's all right – she's still breathing,' said Laura, bashing the soil off.

They took the pig inside where Laura filled the washing-up bowl with water and tipped in some Daz. Prudence emerged looking pinker than ever, very soggy and oozing a lot of bubbles.

'Giving her a bath, then?' Their mother came in with a paint tray full of messy brushes. 'Hurry up – need to give these a soak. Hang her out on the line.'

'Perhaps you'll listen to *me* next time,' said Laura as they carried out the dripping pig. 'That's twice now Sadie's made me look an idiot. Why are you letting her boss you around?'

Sarah wore an expression which was part sorry, and part defiant. 'I'm not allowed to *tell.*'

'Listen, Sarah. This is serious. It's not a game. Please – tell Mum.'

Sarah frowned. 'But I promised. Anyway, I told them, didn't I? I told them she was real. And they didn't believe me. And *you* told me not to tell. You'll get into more trouble if I say you've been telling me Sadie's real again.'

There was a loud clatter from the direction of the fence. Mrs White appeared over the top. She surveyed the garden, clambered down and made her way to the house. Laura knew Sadie had gone. For the moment anyway.

'Thanks, Mrs White,' whispered Laura. 'You're a very good ghost alarm – know that?' They followed the cat inside.

'Where have all the custard creams gone? I only bought a new packet this morning,' said Mrs Logan.

'Sadie had them,' said Nick, strolling in.

'Sadie can't eat biscuits. It makes her sad,' said Sarah.

'I don't want to hear any more about Sadie,' sighed their mother.

'What's for dinner – I'm starving,' said Nick.

Chapter Nine

In the relaxed state of sleep or waking, the senses are
particularly sensitive to paranormal experience.
THE HANDBOOK OF HAUNTINGS

'Here you are, Nick.' Mrs Logan took a note from her
purse. 'Your lucky day! You get to choose. Go to the
Spar and find something for dinner.'

'Me?' said Nick. 'Are you sure you've got the right
person?'

'You eat, don't you? Go on – go and choose something
nice, something quick and easy. And I need a dozen first-
class stamps from the post office. Oh, and the *Evening
Chronicle*. There's the shopping bag.'

'I'm not carrying *that*. Anyway I've only just got in.'

'Well – you can just go out again. And take Sarah with
you while I get on.'

'What? But I don't know anything about shopping.'

'Go!'

Nick shrugged. Like a non-swimmer might shrug,
forced to swim the English Channel without armbands.
He trudged off with Sarah trailing behind him.

Laura went into the sitting room and turned on the
television. Mrs White, dozing on an armchair, yawned,

crawled on to Laura's lap and after much kneading and circling settled down again. Laura was flicking channels when her mother appeared with her father in tow, wiping his hands on a rag. Her mother bent and switched off the television.

'Laura – it's time we had a talk,' said her father.

Uh-oh – here we go, Laura thought. So that's why Mum sent Nick out.

Mr Logan sat in the armchair. Her mother perched on the arm. She clasped her hands together.

'Look, Laura, we know this move has been upsetting for you – and it's probably much more of a wrench for you because of Natalie. After all you have been friends since you were tiny—'

'It's not easy – we know that,' interrupted her father. 'I mean – I can't help feeling a little anxious myself about starting afresh. New people, new place – all of that. We know how you must feel, Laura.'

Laura concentrated on rubbing Mrs White's head.

'But you'll make friends when you start your new school,' said her mother.

'Of course you will,' added her father.

Get to the point, thought Laura. Let's get it over with.

'The point is – well – you don't need to – to...' Her mother's voice trailed off.

'...to try and get our attention this way.' Her father finished the sentence. 'All this talk and hinting about ghosts. They don't exist – whatever they may tell you on the telly. Sadie is just pure imagination on Sarah's part. And yours too.' He shifted his position in the chair. 'But we *do*

96

understand that you're not too happy at the moment. Nick's managed to make a friend quickly. And Sarah's always been good at occupying herself. But – well – we're worried. It's gone beyond a joke now. And it's not very healthy. Especially for Sarah. It might seem funny to you but it's getting out – correction – *got* out of hand.'

'Hold on,' said Laura. 'It's Sarah who goes on and on about Sadie – I didn't invent her.'

'Yes, but what's perfectly normal for a five-year-old, for a girl of nearly thirteen is – well...' He tapped the arm of the chair. 'Well – frankly – it's rather worrying.'

Laura sat slumped into the sofa staring at Mrs White's ear.

'But you do it! And Mum! She was blaming *Sadie* for leaving toothpaste round the basin.'

'That was just a joke, Laura,' said her mother. 'Just a game – going along with Sarah's make-believe friend. You don't seem to know the difference. I mean that business this afternoon. Inventing a story that Sadie was making Sarah cut Prudence up? That was just nasty. You're going too far. Can't you see that?'

'I didn't make that up – I told you – I found Sarah with the knife in the garden. She could have cut herself.'

'But you couldn't leave it at that, could you, Laura?' her mother asked. 'You had to bring *Sadie* into it again – Sadie as some evil influence. You'll be giving Sarah nightmares if you're not careful.'

'It all comes from this rubbish you see in films and television these days,' said her father. He paused. 'Look – we know it's all a bit boring for you at the moment, Laura.

Tell you what – why don't we take an afternoon off sometime, eh? Take a trip to Wookey Hole or...'

Laura tugged at Mrs White's fur. She opened an eye in protest. I don't believe this, she told herself. Sarah can play all day with an invisible girl and chatter on and on about her. And it's OK for Nick to talk to insects with pinhead brains. But *I'm* the one they're worried about? And I'm not playing a game – it's serious.

'...and your mum says Natalie might come for a few days at the end of the holidays? That's something to look forward to, isn't it?'

Laura looked up. 'Yeah – thanks.'

'Right, that's an end to it,' said her father getting up. 'Let's forget all about it.' He gave her knee an encouraging pat. 'Just give it time, eh? You'll settle in.'

'Mum?' said Laura.

'Yes?'

'What's diphtheria?'

Her mother looked puzzled. 'Diphtheria? A disease – a lot of children used to die from it. Before immunisation, that is. When the throat swells up and it's difficult to breathe. Why?'

'Just wondered.'

There was a shout from the hall. 'Mum! What am I supposed to do what this stuff?' Nick burst in. He had a glass in one hand, a rim of milk round his mouth, and a Mars Bar in the other. 'I'm back,' he said.

'Meat pie – yuk,' muttered Laura, picking up the empty packet from the table. She set out the plates and cutlery.

'Am I supposed to set a place for Sadie-the-invisible-girl or not?' she asked, hand on hip.

'I don't think she's coming. But she might be upset if you don't,' said Sarah.

'Yes or no, Sarah.'

'Mmmm – yes.'

Laura made a face at her mother. A sort of 'well-don't-blame-me-I'm-only-doing-what-I'm-told' face.

Mrs Logan was peering into the milk jug. 'Oh dear,' she said.

Laura and Nick jostled to look.

'Ugh!' said Laura.

'Oh no,' groaned Nick.

'Let me see! Let me see!' demanded Sarah.

A large green insect floated in the milk.

'It's Mrs Twiglet – my champion egg layer. She must have escaped with Arnold. Why did it have to be you? It's tragic,' said Nick.

'Ugh,' repeated Laura. 'You drank that. You drank the milk she drowned in. There's probably some of her eggs floating around – and you drank them.'

'Shut up, you – this is all your fault anyway!'

Their father told them both to shut up and sit down.

'Anyway – it's no different from eating meat,' said Laura. 'Probably a lot healthier. I don't know how you can eat that stuff. It's totally disgusting.'

'It's very good,' said their father chewing. 'Good choice, Nick – you can get this again.'

Their mother's expression said she didn't agree but she wasn't going to say so.

'I love meat pie,' said Sarah.

'Meat is dead animals, Sarah,' said Laura. 'Dead cow and dead pig – that's what you're eating. All the nasty bits they scrape off the bones.'

'Lovely,' said Nick.

'They mix it with the blood in special machines to make sausages and pie fillings...'

'Laura!' warned her father.

But Laura couldn't stop. All her anger and frustration bubbled up. '...and the sausages and pies get wrapped up and go to the shops – then on to your plate. Piggy sausages. And piggy pie...'

'*Stop!*' Her father dropped his knife and fork.

There was silence. Except for the sound of Sarah spitting out a mouthful of pie.

Nick leant back and said, 'Delicious.'

'I don't want to eat little piggy pie,' Sarah whined.

'You've completely ruined a perfectly good meal!' cried Mr Logan, pushing back his chair. 'I'm going to finish the painting.'

Nick sat smugly, wagging a finger at Laura as if saying, 'Naughty, naughty.' Mrs Logan glared at Laura. There was a tapping at the window. Shane grinned in.

'It's your friend Noddy,' said Laura to Nick.

Nick got up to leave.

'Hey, Nick!' called Laura, picking up his plate. It had a pea on it. 'I think you've left something behind. Your brain!'

'That's enough, Laura!' snapped her mother. 'I thought we'd come to an understanding! Why do you *always* have to stir things up?' She scraped the plates into the bin.

Nick returned with Shane and showed him his stick insect floating in the milk jug.

'Just get rid of it, please!' ordered Mrs Logan.

Holding the jug ceremonially before him like an offering, Nick slow marched out to the garden, humming a funereal tune. *Dum dum di-dum, dum di-dum-di-dum-di-dum.* Sarah slipped off her chair and ran after them. Laura followed at a distance. Nick progressed slowly down the garden where Shane tried scraping a hole with his hands. Sarah ran to fetch the little trowel.

'You have to sing something – like "All Things Bright and Beautiful",' she informed Nick.

'Yeah – all creatures green and small,' added Laura.

Nick ignored her. He tipped the jug and poured. 'Return to the earth, oh Pamela, layer of eggs,' he intoned. 'And may your spirit live forever on the Great Twig in the Sky.'

'Amen,' said Shane.

The milk splashed into the soil. Nick peered into the jug. 'She's got stuck – give me that spade.'

He scraped her out, just as Mrs White arrived, sniffing at the milky soil. He pushed the cat away. 'Get off! You're not having her too!'

'Anyone seen Sarah?' asked Mr Logan an hour or so later. Mrs Logan had gone to bed with a bad headache.

'Dad! I think you'd better come up here!' called Nick from the attic floor.

They found her in the attic room that Nick had bagged for himself. Her dress and face and hands were smeared with bright yellow paint. She was clasping a dripping paint brush. The newly plastered wall was covered with huge yellow noughts and crosses games. Drips of yellow trailed from the tin to the wall. Their father stared, shaking his head. He took off his glasses, wiped them and put them back on again.

'Sarah – did you do this?' he asked slowly, waving a hand at the mess and the dripped paint. 'Look at this! Just look! This is very, very naughty!'

Sarah chewed her lip. 'Sadie said...'

'Have you been putting ideas into her head again?' demanded their father, turning to Laura.

'No way!' she replied. She would have flounced out if she hadn't been so curious to hear what Sarah had to say.

'You know that isn't true, Sarah,' he said sternly. Well, well, well...' He shook his head again. 'I am very surprised. And very cross, Sarah. Not just about the paint. But about telling fibs. And you have just told me a really big fib. I'm very disappointed in you, Sarah. And very shocked. You know very well, we mustn't tell fibs, must we?'

Sarah straightened her face, glanced sideways, and said, 'No, Daddy. Sorry, Daddy.'

Laura tried ringing Natalie, but she was out. She always seemed to be out these days. That night Laura took her ghost alarm (Mrs White) to bed with her. She wondered why she hadn't thought of it before. Sarah was fast asleep. Mrs White, accustomed to being shut out in the back hall with nothing more than her basket and a bowl of water was immediately suspicious. She darted under Nick's bed out of reach. Laura had to lay a trail of Brekkies to entice her out and on to her bed. After several disturbed nights, and with the comforting weight of Mrs White at her feet, Laura had fallen asleep by the time Nick came upstairs. She was jolted awake by the sensation of someone sitting on her chest. It took several seconds to realise that the pink blob in front of her face was Mrs White's nose.

'Oh – it's you,' she mumbled, pushing her away. She glanced at Nick's clock. Thirteen minutes past five. She'd been dreaming again – about this room. The images were still vivid in her mind. There'd been a table under the window. And a big chest of drawers in the alcove by the fireplace. She looked towards Nick. His bed stood against the fireplace. Boarded up now, just a mantelshelf painted dark green jutting over the bedhead.

Mrs White jumped down and clawed at the door. Laura groaned, let her out and stumbled back to bed. She lay gazing up at the ceiling, trying to remember. A stream of disconnected images flashed in her head. Lacing up a boot. Looking down at the garden from this window: manicured lawns, Sadie on a swing hanging from the big tree. Then sitting at the table under the window, painting a picture – a bird or something. A yellow satin quilt on the bed. Opening the door to a cupboard. She sat up. Hiding something in the cupboard – the one on the other side of the fireplace.

Laura slid out of bed and crept over to look. Nick's bags were piled at the bottom of the cupboard. She dragged them out: his football kit, his judo stuff, some smelly socks, a dirty T-shirt... Carefully, quietly, she removed them, exposing the floorboards beneath. There was a short piece in the corner. It lifted easily. She peered in at the dark space below. She couldn't see anything at first. Then she spotted something. She put in her hand and lifted it out. A small tobacco tin. She prised the lid up. It swung back on little hinges. Inside lay two cigarettes and a box of matches. This is incredible, she thought. I've seen this tin before – in that dream about the den near the railway. But the matches were different. Did Gus pinch these from his father too? He must have done. She held the tin to her nose, a faint stale smell of tobacco still lingered. Gus held this tin, she thought. He hid it – and carried it in his pocket. And now I'm holding it. Even as she cupped it in her hands, the image of the den and its softy mossy floor flickered in her mind. She could almost smell the damp earthy scent of it. But, if I told Nick, I can just imagine what he'd say. Yeah? So you found some crummy old tin – so what?

Laura closed the tin and silently returned everything to the cupboard. She lay in bed thinking about it all. Gazing round the room, looking at the walls. They seemed to look back at her. You've seen all that's happened in this room, she thought. You've seen Gus and Sadie. And now you can see us. I wonder if one day there'll be memories of us left behind.

Hi Nat – it's me. I tried ringing you last night AND this morning but you weren't there were you? And

Dad caught me so I got THE LECTURE about the cost of daytime calls. Did you get my other letter yet? I reckon it got pinched – by our ghost. The line going dead the other evening was her too. Of course no one believes me. She's a girl called Sadie – Mum and Dad think she's just Sarah's make-believe friend. I've not actually seen her – except in these weird dreams I keep having. But she's definitely there – tho not all the time. You believe me don't you? Say you believe me Nat!!

Laura read back her letter and sighed. It read like a practical joke but it would have to do. Half an hour ago Natalie's mother had told her over the phone that Natalie was staying at Shelley's for a few days. Laura had felt hurt and let down and angry all at the same time. She gazed round the room. The bed had been there – the wardrobe over there. It had felt so real. She chewed on the pen, looked down at the blank paper and added:

Mum says you can come and stay at the end of the holidays

Laura threw the pad on the pile of clothes on her chair. She'd write the rest later, when she was in a better mood. She slid off the bed and went downstairs to look for an envelope. Her mother was in the hall, chatting to a woman who had a little girl with her. A baby in a pushchair was parked by the front door. Sarah and the girl eyed one another silently. Laura tried to slip past unnoticed.

'Oh – and here's my other daughter, Laura – she'll be thirteen next week. Laura – this is Mrs Russell, and this is Becky. We got chatting in the post office the other day,' her mother explained. 'Becky has invited Sarah to play today. Isn't that nice?'

The two girls continued to stare silently at one another. Laura slipped away.

Chapter Ten

Of course, in a state of heightened anxiety,
imagination can play tricks on the human mind.
THE HANDBOOK OF HAUNTINGS

As Laura walked back into the kitchen it went quiet. Her mother immediately began to act busy with the dishcloth. Nick, leaning against a cupboard stared moodily down at the floor. Shane, hands in pockets, wobbled his head at her.

'Well – I'd better be getting on,' said Mrs Logan and throwing a look at Nick, left.

Nick watched his mother go, then said to the floor, 'If you're bored you can come with us. Only if you like. You don't *have* to,' he emphasised, glancing up at Laura.

'Yeah. Okey-dokes with me,' bobbed Shane cheerily.

'Unless you've got something better to do?' said Nick hopefully.

Laura looked from one to the other. So this is what Mum was fixing. Getting Nick to feel sorry for poor lonely me. Flipping cheek. I bet she bribed him.

'As it happens I have loads of better things to do,' she said as she started to address her envelope at the kitchen table.

Nick cheered up visibly and prised himself from the cupboard. 'Come on then, Shane. Let's go.'

'On the other hand...' said Laura, her boredom getting the better of her.

'Make your mind up,' Nick complained. He slouched towards the door. 'Come on then – if you're coming.'

'Where are you going?' she demanded.

'Dunno yet, do we?' beamed Shane. 'We let the fates guide us, don' we, Nick?'

'Bring your bike – we'll meet you out the front,' Nick said.

The fates, it seemed were telling Nick and Shane to turn left along Storrington Road, away from the centre of the village. Laura pedalled behind them. Shane turned left again.

'Come on! Come on! Keep up!' yelled Nick.

Shane stopped outside a row of stone cottages. He signalled to Laura to be quiet. The cottages were fronted by long narrow gardens. All but one were clearly visible from the road. But the garden of the end cottage was enclosed by a thick hedge of trees and bushes. The laurels on either side of the gate, overtaken by ivy, almost met in the middle. Shane had propped up his bike and was half bent, head craning from side to side, trying to peer in.

He beckoned. 'Want to see a witch?' he said in a low voice.

Laura, seeing Nick's smirking face, dismissed this with a look that said, 'grow up'. She sighed, then squinted through the hedge. All she could see was the slated roof and a wilderness of weeds and nettles.

'Isn't it supposed to be made of icing and marzipan sweets?' she mocked, peering over the gate.

'Sssh! Want 'er to see us?' said Shane, pulling her down.

'Yeah – she'll turn you into a frog if you're not careful,' Nick muttered.

'She's down there all right – saw her come out 'er front door there. I reckon she's collectin' stuff for one of her potions. Snails and spit and stuff. Hocus pocus puke and snot – your eyes'll pop your nose'll rot,' chanted Shane under his breath.

Nick was crouched, shaking with giggles, struggling to smother them. Laura stared at him. My *mature* brother, she thought. She squinted down the garden again.

'There's no one there. Come on – let's go,' she said.

'Just stay down will you!' hissed Nick.

She sank back on her heels again.

'Everyone round 'ere knows about ol' Mrs Quigley,' whispered Shane. 'She's a weird one, she is. She does make potions – no kidding. Pete Johnson's dad 'ad one – wouldn't tell us what for – just he was desperate. Said it smelt somethin' dreadful. And my brother broke in once – for a dare like. Never again, he said. It was well creepy. Said there were these great big eyes starin' at him out of the wall. Couldn't get out fast enough, could he?'

Shane bobbed his head over the gate. 'Come on,' he beckoned. He scuttled along to the hedge of the meadow that bordered on to the garden and squeezed himself through. Nick and Laura followed.

'Brian Fudge saw her boilin' things up in a cauldron once,' he confided. 'He swears she dropped in a cat's tail,' he breathed. 'Ginger it was. And guess what? His ginger cat had just gone missin', 'adn't it?'

'Had it?'

Shane nodded solemnly.

Laura swallowed. Hunched over, Shane led them along the hedge, where he suddenly dropped to his haunches and peered through. He withdrew slowly and signalled with a finger to his lips. Crouching beside him, Laura and Nick craned to find a spyhole in the hedge. Laura could hear a low muttering. Suddenly she caught a glimpse of an old woman. She was stooped over, poking at something under the bushes, talking to herself. Despite the hot weather, she was wearing an old brown raincoat. Her hair, startlingly white and spiky, bristled from beneath a red beret. A large purple flower was sticking out of it. Laura couldn't see her face. Only a bony hand clasping a large saucepan.

'Ha! Got you!' she muttered and threw something into it.

Laura glanced at Shane. He bobbed a look of 'See – didn't I tell you?'

'Slugs and spiders,' he whispered. 'She's gonna boil 'em alive. Watch this.'

He scrabbled around for a handful of earth, darted a look through the hedge, then jumped up and hurled the earth over. It landed with a spattering sound and the old woman's head jerked up. She squinted in the direction of the sound, then straightened up, turned and stared right at them as if the hedge was transparent. They froze. Shane looked strangely immobile with his bobbing head still for once. The old woman glanced away and shuffled back towards the cottage. Nick grabbed a pebble and hurled that over too. It rebounded off a flowerpot with a ping. The three of them crouched beneath the hedge, their nerves giving way to convulsive laughter, hands over mouths, shaking silently.

Suddenly, from the hedge, the fork came thrusting out at them, held by a bony hand. They fell back, Nick and Shane wide-eyed with shock, Laura giving an involuntary shriek.

'I know you're there! Don't think I can't see you! I know you, my lad! I know where you live!' screeched the old woman. The fork jabbed towards Shane. 'And the girl!'

Laura shrank back from the hedge. She saw the red beret and the white hair.

'Oh yes! I know you, Laura! I know you, Laura!' she threatened as they leapt up and ran.

Grabbing their bikes, they jumped on, pedalling furiously without looking back. The road suddenly steepened and they had to stand on the pedals. Nick looked backed, urging Laura on with a hand signal, pointing down to the right, over a low stone wall. She caught the boys up and saw that they were standing on a bridge. Shane climbed over and Nick passed the bikes over the wall to him. He was standing at the top of a steep bank, sloping down to a flat grassy area. They clambered over and joined Shane, carefully easing their way down the bank with their bikes, panting to get their breath back when they reached the bottom.

'She knew my name! She knew my name! How did she know that?' struggled Laura between breaths. She was scared. More than she cared to admit.

'Told you she was a witch,' Shane gasped, leaning over his handlebars.

'I didn't even do anything!'

'Look – she's not really a witch,' shrugged Nick. 'I mean – there's no such thing. Is there, Shane? Shane?'

'Nah – nah – course not.'

'She must have heard one of us say it,' said Nick. 'Don't worry about it – she's just an old woman – a loony.'

'Yeah – that's right,' nodded Shane. 'Forget about it, eh?'

'Unless of course you start to hop and croak and turn green,' joked Nick.

It's all right for you, Laura thought. She didn't even seem to notice you.

They set off away from the bridge along a rough grassy path, hemmed in on either side by trees and bushes on rising banks.

She knew my name, thought Laura. She knew my name.

'This used to be the railway line – in the olden days like. Used to go through the village,' called Shane.

'What! What did you say!' said Laura, braking.

'What's up now?' called Nick, stopping.

'Shane said something – about this being an old railway line.'

Shane turned. 'Yeah – it was. Ages ago, like. All those little bridges go over where it used to run.'

'Come on – let's go,' urged Nick.

Laura followed, lost in thought, remembering her dream: running along the railway track, the black

112

chimney... It's more than coincidence, she thought. More than a dream too.

The banks on either side loomed higher and closed in. She felt as if she were travelling in a green tunnel. The light cast a greenish glow on her hands gripping the handlebars and on her pistoning knees. She felt like a large frog. She glanced at Nick and Shane. They both looked green too.

'Look,' she called, trying to make light of it. 'Look – we're turning green. We're turning into frogs already.'

'Croak, croak,' said Nick. Then he raced off.

Laura imagined them growing greener and smaller. Soon their feet wouldn't reach the pedals. Their hands would shrink into those tiny blobby fingers. They would hop away to find a shady place. Their three bikes lying where they had toppled. Policemen with tracker dogs would search every inch of path. While three little frogs would look on helplessly, crying, 'Here we are! Here we are!' Only it would come out as, 'Croak croak croak.' It would be one of those unsolved disappearances. There might even be a television programme about it. No more cheese on toast. Just flies and – well – whatever frogs liked to eat. Ugh.

The green light shimmered. The heat rose from the ground. Insects darted and buzzed. The wheels of the bikes whirred. The tunnel stretched endlessly ahead. The moment took on a strange dreamy quality. What was happening to her? Well, at least it's taken my mind off Sadie, she thought. No it hasn't. Her thoughts darted from Sadie to Mrs Quigley to frogs and back to her dream. It was ended abruptly by a cloud of dust as Nick executed a fancy swerving brake.

But then, off to the right, rising from the side of a sloping hill, a small mountain came into view. Covered in fir trees, conical, its point jutted sharply above the skyline of soft curves of the hills.

'What's that funny little mountain?' shouted Laura, trying to take her mind off things.

'That's an ol' slag heap, that is. You know – where they dumped all the waste. Rocks and earth'n stuff from the mines,' shouted Shane.

'What mines? You never told me anything about mines,' shouted Nick.

They pedalled along slowly, three abreast.

'In the olden days – used to be coal mines, din't there? All round 'ere. The Somerset Coal Field, wasn't it? That's where the pithead used to be – near the slag heap. We did that in the juniors. Fancy you not knowing that. My granddad remembers 'em. His dad was a carting boy. He used to haul the coal trucks. One ha'penny a ton he used to get. Can you believe that? One ha'penny a ton.' Shane's head wobbled in disbelief. 'I'm dyin' for a lolly,' he added.

He led them on, down a narrow corkscrew hill, between steep green banks and old yellow stone walls. Beyond them an undulating blanket of patches, all shades of greens and yellows, stitched together with dark hedges. The dipping curves revealed the jut of a roof or the glint of a window.

These old walls and cottages must have been there for ages, Laura thought. And Sadie and Gus might have come here. She could see Gus on his bike. A sturdy black bike. Fearlessly swooping down, Sadie behind him, her pigtails streaming behind her. What a weird day this is, she thought. What's happening to me?

The lane zig-zagged sharply and grew steeper. The air whistled and beat her face, blowing away all thoughts. She whizzed downhill, faster and faster, everything a blur. Nick and Shane had disappeared round a bend. She caught them up, released her brakes and flew past them. The road levelled, then rose and twisted into a street of cottages and houses and a small church. An ice-cream sign on a narrow pavement came into view. She stopped and waited for them. They bought ices and sat on the church wall to eat them.

'Did you see 'er cauldron?' said Shane.

'It was a saucepan,' said Laura, wishing he would talk about something else.

'Same thing, same thing,' bobbed Shane. 'It's what she puts in it that counts.'

They set off again, turning down a track alongside a narrow brook. They followed it along a devious route, led by Shane, eventually coming out again on the main road. Laura was surprised to see how close to home they were, the tower of the church and the roof of Hillview House clearly visible. She was astonished to see that they had been out for over four hours.

Mr Logan was piling rubbish on to a bonfire at the bottom of the garden when Laura and Nick reached home. Their old bath and basin had been dumped outside.

'Well – what do you think, folks?' said their mother to them both as they walked into the kitchen.

The room was transformed from its former gloom. The cupboards had been painted blue. Brass knobs had been added. The walls were a sunny yellow. Dark red tiles glowed on the floor where the old covering had been removed.

'It's a bit yellow,' said Nick.

'No, it's nice,' said Laura.

A paint-stained sheet of newspaper on the table, skidded as a sudden gust blew in. Somewhere upstairs a door slammed loudly.

'It's been doing that all day – shut the back door, Nick,' their mother said.

Sarah arrived home from Becky's house. 'Becky kept making empty faces,' she told Laura. 'All the things I wanted to play she just made an empty face. Like this.' Sarah demonstrated a long bored expression. 'She showed me her guinea pig though. Except it wasn't there. Just its empty hutch and little fence thingy round an old cabbage. Then we had to look for it. Then she started to cry. Then I came home.' She did a handstand against the fridge. 'And they've got three toilets. I liked the pink one best.'

Mrs Logan was stuffing a bin bag with paint-stained newspapers and rags to take down to the bonfire. As she went out to the garden the door slammed behind her.

'Here, Sarah,' said Laura, tearing off a sheet of paper from her pad and fetching a box of crayons. 'Why don't you draw a picture for Natalie? I'll put in it with my letter – she'd like that. How about a picture of Sadie?' she whispered.

Sarah sat down at the table and began to draw. A sudden draught of air lifted the paper from the table. Sarah slapped it down but the paper seemed to have a life of its own. It tore itself free and shot upwards. The draught of air became a cold whirling gust, swirling the paper above them. They stared up at it, mouths open in astonishment. As suddenly as it had entered, the gust exited through the hall door, the paper fluttering slowly down. Sarah ran out to the hall, Laura charging behind her. Loose strips of wallpaper flapped as the gust tore upstairs. A door slammed again. They raced up, past the bathroom, where Mr Samson was singing along loudly to his radio. Their bedroom door was shut. They looked at one another then rushing at the door, fell in. Nick looked up from his bed.

'Oh no – not you,' he said. 'Can't I get any peace? First it's doors slamming, now it's you. I'm going.' He picked up his computer magazine and sloped off.

Behind them the door slammed shut. The light bulb began to swing. Gently at first, then faster. The air gathered speed around them.

Chapter Eleven

Poltergeist: German for 'noisy spirit'. Capable of throwing and lifting and moving heavy objects. Sometimes in association with other paranormal activity.
THE HANDBOOK OF HAUNTINGS

Laura snatched Sarah's hand. 'Come on!' she cried, running for the door. But it wouldn't open. No matter how she pulled and tugged, it stuck fast.

The light bulb was whirling furiously now, the air spiralling above them, sucking in clothes and toys and other items, like a tornado. They felt themselves being sucked in, backwards, towards the wall. Now they were pinned against it. Helpless, unable to move as everything swirled. Quite suddenly, it petered out and they fell to the floor. Objects showered down on them as they crouched, arms over their heads. At last it became still. Laura reached for Sarah.

'It's Sadie, isn't it!' she whispered 'Can you see her?'

Sarah, looking pale and tearful, shook her head.

Laura tried the door again. It wouldn't open. Now she was really scared but trying not to let Sarah see how much. She perched on the edge of the bed, her arm around Sarah, glancing anxiously around the room. The silent stillness of the room was intense. But Sadie hadn't finished. Only thinking what to do next. The bed suddenly tilted, sending Laura sprawling backwards. The mattress began to heave. She clung on as it rippled and rolled, like a boat shooting the rapids. Then, with an enormous lurch it tipped her on to the floor.

'I'm all right – I'm all right,' she reassured Sarah, getting to her feet. 'See – didn't I tell you – Sadie's not nice,' she added under her breath. 'Now will you believe me...'

Nick's radio blared on at deafening volume, drowning her voice. Then Nick's belt, hanging from the bed, reared, snaked across the floor and lunged at Laura. She screamed and leapt on the bed. Then grabbing Sarah, she rushed to the window. It slammed down.

'Mum! Dad!' Laura screamed through the glass as she struggled to tug it open. The radio blared louder. She could see smoke from the bonfire rising behind the greenhouse and caught a glimpse of her father's back and her mother tossing something on to the fire.

'Dad! Dad!' she yelled again, banging on the window.

She glanced back at the room. Sarah was now standing in the centre, clutching her pig to her chest. Like a miniature Rumpelstiltskin, she stamped her foot and cried, 'Stop it, stop it, stop it! Or I won't be friends any more! I don't like it!'

Beneath the noise, another noise now. Someone banging on the door.

'What's going on in there! Open up!' they heard Nick yell.

Instantly there was a tiny but perceptible shift of mood

in the room. As if pausing for thought. Then, as the radio blared, like a film rewinding, the objects that had been hurled around the room rose and reversed to their original places. Within seconds everything was as it had been before. The door suddenly flung open and Nick fell in. He looked at them with fierce curiosity and suspicion.

'What are you two playing at? Making enough noise weren't you? And who said you could use my radio?' He crossed the room and turned it off. The sudden silence fell like a cold wet wave.

'Well?' he demanded.

Sarah threw a secret questioning look at Laura. Laura felt as if she was choking. She wanted to let it all spill out, but a picture of Nick's mocking face flashed into her head. She saw her parents' expressions of irritation. They would not believe a word of it. And, looking at the room now, who would blame them? Just the usual disorder produced by three children and their clutter sharing a room. No clues at all to the turmoil of only a few minutes ago.

'Mind your own business,' she said.

'You were playing *my* radio – that *is* my business.'

He fetched his camera from his drawer then turned back to the door. 'How did you do that? Jam a chair under it or something? Come on – tell me. What's going on?'

He left without getting an answer. An exhausted but smouldering stillness filled the room.

'She's still here, isn't she?' said Laura under her breath. 'Where is she, Sarah?'

Sarah had been glancing towards her bed. There was a sense of sullen silence, as if Sarah's threat had taken Sadie by surprise. Also Nick's interruption. As if Sadie was re-thinking her tactics. Laura knew now, without a doubt, that Sadie was determined that no one else should suspect her presence. Or believe any talk of ghosts. She looked at Sarah, who was scowling at the bed.

'I never! Not a proper promise. You made me!' Sarah burst out. Then she stood frowning as if listening. '...and they don't go throwing people's things around – you could have hurt us you could – and it was frightening and...' Sarah continued.

Suddenly Prudence Pig was jerked from her grasp and began to somersault in mid-air. Sarah tried to grab Prudence back but the toy swooped and dived round the room like some sort of superpig. As it somersaulted along the bed, Sarah's expression softened. When the pig did the splits, stood on its head, sprang to its feet and took a bow, Sarah smiled. When the pig started to play hide and seek behind the pillow, Sarah giggled.

Laura watched in amazement. Sadie's clever, she thought. I've got to admit she's clever. Really clever. It's almost as if it never happened. Look – she's got round Sarah again. By distracting her, by making her laugh.

A long pause now as Laura watched Sarah listening to Sadie.

'All right,' she sighed. 'But only if you promise not to do it again.'

'Tell me what's going on,' Laura demanded. 'What's she saying, Sarah?'

Sarah took a deep breath. 'She was very sad and got cross,' she said, going to her bed and reaching for

122

Prudence. ''Cos she was left on her own – and I wasn't here – and she wanted to play. She's been waiting all day. And once she started she couldn't stop...' Sarah tried to make her pig somersault. '...but she wouldn't hurt anyone,' she said. Not really. And she's promised not to do it again. She says she's sorry.'

'If you believe that, you'll believe anything,' Laura thought. Best let her think I'm going along with it, though. Don't give my thoughts away.

'And she did tidy it all up again,' said Sarah, as if that excused it all. She turned away from Laura, stroking Prudence's ears, as if Laura was no longer there. 'It was really boring at Becky's,' Sarah explained to the pillow. 'I like playing with you best. Can we play weddings? Or mothers and fathers? Not hospitals. I'm fed up of hospitals.'

Laura pictured Sadie sitting cross-legged opposite her. Tossing her plaits over her shoulders. The feeling of fury in the room had disappeared. Two little girls were playing. Only one of them was a ghost-child. A seven-year-old child who had been around for eighty years. The sense of her in the room was overpowering. Wilful, dominating, manipulative and – full of life. How could a ghost be full of life?

'Here comes the bride – all fat and wide,' sang Sarah, walking Prudence up her bed cover.

Laura focused on the spot where she guessed Sadie was sitting. 'Sarah – ask her whose room this used to be? What's she say, Sarah?'

'Gus's. It was Gus's room.'

Laura gasped. 'Gus's? And was the bed over there – and was there a yellow silky sort of quilt?' she said excitedly. 'And a big wardrobe there and a table...?'

Sarah glanced from Laura to Sadie and nodded her head.

'I dreamt that – this is really weird. And there was a swing, wasn't there? On that big tree?'

Sarah looked at the pillow, then nodded again at Laura.

'Ask her what happened – why was she waiting for Gus – what happened...?'

'We're trying to play, Laura!' complained Sarah. 'Can you stop talking please? She's been waiting all day to play you know.'

'But I'd like to know why she keeps having a go at me and causing trouble and—'

'It's only *joking*.'

'And I suppose letting Nick's insects out was a joke too, was it?'

Sarah listened patiently, head on one side as Sadie explained.

'She says – 'scuse me but that was just an accident – she didn't mean to – only they were so horrid. She only wanted a peek – but they made her jump and she dropped the lid – and they were too disgusting to pick up – and she's very sorry – and she won't ever touch them again. Not with a disinfected bargepole thank you very much.'

'Why are you here then, Sadie? What...'

Sarah dropped Prudence, folded her arms and said huffily, 'You made her go now. She won't come back. Not till you've gone. Go away, Laura – we want to *play*.'

'I don't think you should...'

Sarah clasped her hands over her ears and sang, 'I'm not listening, I'm not listening...'

Laura shook her head in frustration and wandered out on to the landing. As the door closed behind her she heard Sarah giggling. She waited, straining to hear. It was no use. She slowly climbed to the attic rooms. There was a small stepladder beneath the open window. She sat on it, staring out at the sky.

So – Sadie had been furious at being left on her own all day. She was not only demanding, but very jealous. Look, she's only a little girl, Laura tried to reassure herself. A lost little girl. OK – she's a little girl. But she's a *dangerous* little girl.

Laura knew that Sadie was growing stronger day by day. She could sense it. Her visits lengthier. Her personality filling out. A dominating presence. Mischievous. Cunning. Jealous.

She really freaked out there, didn't she? Laura thought. And if she could do it once, she could do it again. How much longer can I take this? The thought of Sadie watching her every move, airing an opinion, playing her games, was appalling. That's why Sadie's become more secretive, Laura realised. She wants Sarah all to herself. She doesn't want anyone interfering – and that's why she doesn't like me. So she's fixed it so it looks as if I'm making it all up. She wants everyone to think she's only Sarah's imagination. At least Sarah stood up to her. Sort of. But I think Sadie's only just discovering the power she has. What could she do if she really set her mind to it? But it's not just Sarah and Sadie, is it? It's Gus too. I mean that railway track – it wasn't just a dream. It existed. What happened to them both? Laura wondered.

So – what am I going to do? Wait and watch, she told herself. There must be some way of catching her out. Try to get round her, make it look as if I'm sympathetic. Persuade her to go – to wherever she should be.

Laura peered out of the window. To the left she could see the trees behind which she knew the brook ran. Was that really today? Old Mrs Quigley suddenly barged into her head. 'I know you, Laura!' Then Sadie butted in. 'Miss Laura Nosey Parker, you mean.'

'Nosey Parker yourself,' she said out loud.

'What?' Nick stood in the doorway.

'Oh – it's you. Nothing.'

'I've been calling you for ages. Didn't you hear? Mum says do you want three vegi-sausages or four? Or you can have casserole – but it's got chicken in it.'

'Oh no – not vegi-sausages. She knows I hate vegi-sausages.'

'Just tell me – three or four.'

'I can't stand them – I keep telling her.'

'OK, OK – don't get your knickers in a twist. I'll tell her none then.' He turned to leave.

'Hang about – I'm starving. Tell her four – no make it five,' Laura said, remembering she hadn't eaten since breakfast.

Nick looked as if he was about to say something, changed his mind, gave a despairing shrug and went. Laura followed and peered down at him over the banister. Along the landing below, she saw Sarah dancing and twirling towards the stairs, humming a tune, dressed in the bridesmaid's outfit she'd worn at their cousin's wedding. She lifted her eyes to Laura and gave a slow arrogant smile. Then hitched up her skirt and slid down the banister.

As Laura walked into the kitchen, Sarah was gathering up the knife, fork and spoon from the place that was set for Sadie.

'I don't need these any more.' She held them out to Nick.

'Huh?' said Nick, looking up from doodling on the newspaper. 'I've only just put them out – I don't want them. Stupid anyway, I call it.'

'What?' said Laura eagerly. 'Sadie's gone, has she?'

The sense of relief was immediate. As if she'd become lighter, almost floating.

Sarah turned. 'No. *Sadie* hasn't gone. Sarah's gone. I'm *Sadie* now, so everyone has to call me Sadie, right?'

The girl held Laura's startled gaze. Laura stared in horror at Sarah's face. But the child that stared back was not Sarah. It was Sadie. Defiant. Triumphant.

The girl turned and skipped to the small mirror hanging on the wall by the sink. She dragged a chair over and stood on it. Then gazed at herself in the mirror. And smiled.

Chapter Twelve

*Possession: when a spirit enters or inhabits
the body of a living person.*
THE HANDBOOK OF HAUNTINGS

For a few seconds Laura stopped breathing. Her eyes
sending signals of panic and warning at her mother. Then
at Nick. Waiting, expecting – urging some sort of reaction.

'Nutty. Both of them,' scoffed Nick. 'Good job you've
got me, Mum. At least one of us is normal.'

'Quick – out of the way, Nick! This is hot,' said their
mother rushing across from the oven with a dish. 'And tell
your dad – dinner's ready.'

Laura stared desperately at her mother. 'Mum! Didn't
you hear what she just said?'

'Look – move those crayons from the table and take
these potatoes.'

'Dad! Dinner!' yelled Nick through the back door.

'Oh, Sarah, you shouldn't be wearing that dress,' said
their mother, catching sight of Sarah on the chair. 'Not to
play. It'll get spoiled. You make sure you change after
dinner.'

This is a nightmare. Please, someone, tell me this isn't

happening, thought Laura. She turned. 'Go on. Tell her, Sadie. Tell her again. I don't think she could have heard you.'

Without taking her eyes from the mirror where she was absorbed in gazing at herself from different angles, the little girl said, 'I like the name Sadie best, Mummy. So I'm Sadie now.'

'But Sarah's a much prettier name,' said Mrs Logan, searching the draining board. 'It means Princess. Remember? Has anyone seen my big slatted spoon?'

Sadie threw a sly smirk at Laura. Laura opened her mouth to speak. Then shut it. She knew that whatever she said would be a waste of breath. And would get her into deep trouble.

'Did you hear, Daddy?' the little girl said as their father walked in. 'I've got a new name. I'm Sadie now.'

'That's going to make it a bit confusing, isn't it?' said Mr Logan. 'What with your *friend* being Sadie.'

'Nuttier and nuttier,' mumbled Nick.

Sadie climbed down from the chair and, holding out the skirt of her dress, twirled around the table, humming to herself.

'Anyway – Sadie's just a nickname for Sarah. Only it's much nicer. I think it's more beautiful,' she said, pirouetting.

'How come she knows that?' Laura demanded, looking at her mother.

'I just know,' said Sadie. 'Anyway, I feel like a princess. I look like a princess in this dress. Don't you think I look like a princess?' She stroked it lovingly. Her voice, her intonation and the way she held her head to one side, was exactly like Sarah's. She pointed her toes in Sarah's little silver sandals. 'Look – I'm wearing princess shoes too! They make me want to dance. I'm going to dance and dance and dance!' she sang as she pranced and twirled.

'Flipping hell,' said Nick. 'Give it a rest, will you? What's got into you all of a sudden?'

Sadie's got into her, thought Laura as she watched her skip to her chair and sit down. And what about Sarah? Where's Sarah now? What's happened to Sarah?

Laura felt sick with helplessness. She wanted to scream. To leap up from her chair and shake the silly smiles off their faces. She wanted to shout, 'Look – this isn't Sarah! I know it isn't! Do something! We've got to get Sarah back!'

'Everyone want potatoes?' said their mother.

Laura glared at the girl.

'Don't stare. It's rude,' she said.

'OK – if you're Sadie, where's Sarah then?'

'She's having a little rest.'

'When's she coming back?'

'I haven't decided yet.'

'So where is she? Come on. Tell us!'

'What is this, Laura?' joked their father. 'The Spanish Inquisition? Take it easy – it's only a game.'

'Yes, Laura – it's only *pretending*,' beamed Sadie sweetly. 'Don't be cross with her, Daddy. She's just a little bit jealous. She didn't want to move here, did she? And she hasn't got any friends, has she? So we have to be nice to her. Even when she's rude and horrible. I feel quite sorry

131

for her, really,' she sighed. She smiled a pious smile at Laura.

'I think I'm going to be sick,' glowered Laura.

The girl's eyes were now ravenously following the dishing up of food and the passing of plates. She seemed to be devouring it with her eyes. Her little tongue slid between her lips. She almost pounced on the plate as it was set down. Potatoes, peas, chicken casserole disappeared into her eager little mouth. She chewed and swallowed. An expression of rapture spread across her face.

'Slow down, Sarah. It's not a race. Anyone would think you hadn't eaten for a week,' said their mother.

She hasn't, thought Laura. Not for weeks. Or months. Or years. Not for over eighty years.

The girl leant back in her chair with an ecstatic smile. 'That was delicious, Mummy. Thank you, Mummy.' Her voice lingered on the word Mummy. Savouring it. She caught Laura's scowl and sat up. 'Mummy – Laura's been horrible to me today. She keeps making up stories – about ghosts and things. And I don't like it. She goes on and on about how Sadie's a ghost. She's been trying to scare me. I keep telling her Sadie is only pretend. But she won't stop and—'

'That's not true!' Laura broke in as her parents' faces registered irritation.

'I'm warning you, Laura, if I hear one more word about ghosts,' said her father, wagging his fork at her, 'I'll – I'll do something drastic.'

'She was really bossy and grumpy,' Sadie went on. 'She was throwing all my things around the room – I had to

132

clear it all up.' She sat back with a self-righteous sigh.

'What!' Laura protested. 'Mum, Dad, don't believe her!'

'Yeah. I heard all that,' nodded Nick. 'Through the ceiling. Crashing and banging she was. Sounded like World War Three. And she'd jammed the door shut. So that's what it was all about.'

Laura wanted to cry with the injustice of it all. They sat there. All four of them looking at her. Her parents with weary impatience. Nick with gleeful pity. Sadie with an artful smile of angelic sweetness. With sudden insight, Laura saw that this was what Sadie wanted. She wanted her to explode with rage. To demonstrate that she was a girl who over-reacted. Who went over the top. Who fabricated things. Who invented ghosts. And could therefore never be taken quite seriously. Nor be believed.

Laura took a deep breath. And forced herself to laugh. As if it was all a big joke. 'Ha! Well done, Sarah! You really got them going there! Dad – we were making up dances, that's all. We had the radio on but got carried away a bit, crashed into things – and the door. And we didn't want Nick barging in so we jammed it. Then we had this bet. To see who could be the most annoying to each other. And get you believing it was real. And you did. You believed it! OK, Sarah. You win. I lose. That was very good. You could be an actress.'

'Strange sort of game,' said their father.

Sadie looked at her with fury, her gaze almost mesmerising. Laura tore herself away.

'Anyway I'm not grumpy,' she bluffed. 'It was good

133

today. Did Nick tell you? We had this great bike ride. And you've made a great job of the kitchen, Mum. It's brilliant.'

Nick frowned at her with deep suspicion.

Laura pushed away her plate of vegi-sausages. The thought of food made her feel ill. 'Sorry, Mum. I can't eat this – I've pulled a muscle or something. It really hurts.' She clasped her ribs and grimaced.

'Oh dear,' said her mother. 'I thought you were looking a bit pale. Want to go and lie down for a bit?'

'No – I'll be OK. I'll just get a glass of water.'

Nick pointed at her plate and said, 'You're not going to let her get away with that, are you, Mum?'

'Sadie can have them, seeing as she's so greedy,' said Laura.

'She hasn't got tummy ache,' smirked Sadie. 'She's just making it up. She—'

'Game over, Sarah,' interrupted their mother.

'Sadie!' frowned Sadie.

I win. This round anyway, thought Laura. Please, please, please. Let Sarah be OK.

'Who wants ice-cream?' asked Mrs Logan.

Sadie devoured hers greedily.

'Hang about! I haven't even got mine yet,' said Nick.

Sadie demolished a second helping.

'Didn't they feed you at your friend's house? You don't know when to stop, you don't,' said Nick.

'Yes I do,' smiled Sadie. 'When it's all gone.'

There was a crash of the cat flap. Their father had fitted it yesterday. Mrs White growled for their attention. Everyone looked.

'Oh no. Please...' said their mother.

Something furry was hanging from Mrs White's mouth. Something brown and white. She laid it before them as an offering. Then sat down and looked proudly up at them, as if expecting gratitude.

'Hey – it's a guinea pig,' said Nick getting up. He poked it. 'Looks like it's a goner. Where d'you get that from then, Missus?'

But Mrs White was staring at Sarah. She arched her back and backed away, hurling herself out through the cat flap.

'Guilt,' said their father.

'Oh dear. I think I know where this came from,' frowned their mother. 'This must be Becky's. That cat is getting to be too much. Sarah...'

'*Sadie*, Mummy.'

'You're not to breathe a word of this. To Becky – or her mummy.'

Sadie frowned.

She doesn't know what you're talking about, Mum, thought Laura. But Sadie had worked it out.

'Daddy said it's very naughty to tell fibs. Didn't you, Daddy?'

'It's a kind fib,' explained their mother. 'We're fibbing to be kind. She'd be very upset if we told her the truth. Nick – can you...?'

'I ought to be an undertaker,' groaned Nick. 'I'm getting enough practice. Have you noticed how her victims are getting bigger? What's it going to be next? A dog?'

*

Laura followed Sadie up the stairs. Sadie turned. 'Go away,' Sadie ordered. Her eyes bore into Laura, unblinking.

I'm not going to look away, I'm not, Laura's head repeated.

Sadie smiled a contemptuous smile. Laura followed her into the bedroom. She scanned the room looking for signs of Sarah. Her shorts, little canvas shoes and her T-shirt lay on the bed. As if she had evaporated into thin air.

'Miss Busy Body. Miss Nosey Parker,' sang Sadie.

'Where's Sarah? Tell me!'

'Silence in the jungle, silence in the court, you're a big fat monkey, if you're first to talk!' sang Sadie. She attempted a handstand against the wall. She came down clumsily, without Sarah's grace and agility.

'Where is Sarah?'

'You're a big fat monkey!' pointed Sadie, scrambling to her feet.

She started to open drawers. Tugging out tops and socks and jumpers. Held them against herself before the mirror. Then turned her attention to the wardrobe. Pulling things off hangers. Tugging clothes on and off. Trying on Sarah's shoes and slippers. Frantically catching up on eighty years of waiting.

'That's my favourite skirt – you're not having that!' snapped Laura. Then immediately thought, What does it matter? It's Sarah that matters.

Sadie made an *ugh* face and let the skirt drop.

'Sadie – tell me where Sarah is. You'd better not have hurt her!'

The girl ignored her. The floor was now strewn with clothes where she'd tossed them. She stood before the mirror, pulling on Sarah's red sundress and sunhat. Then, hands in the pockets, she turned to admire herself. She drew out something from one of the pockets – Sarah's heart-shaped sunglasses. Excitedly she put them on. Smiled with pleasure at her reflection.

'Tell me where Sarah is!'

'Don't get yourself in a tizzy!' said Sadie without taking her eyes from the mirror. 'She's fine. Oh – don't I look lovely!' Her voice had changed. Sarah's voice had gone. This voice was arrogant, assured. Sadie twirled.

'No. It's Sarah who looks lovely. And you've stolen her. You've got to give her back. Before anything happens to her!' demanded Laura.

Sadie sat down to put on the silver sandals again.

Laura glared at her. 'You know you're dead, don't you, Sadie?'

Sadie looked up.

'I'm not – I'm not!' Then she smiled, 'You can see I'm not.'

'But you are, Sadie. And you shouldn't be here. You have to go. To wherever you should be. And give Sarah back. It's wicked. Really wicked, what you're doing.'

'It's not wicked – I'm good – I'm a good girl, I am! I'm not hurting Sarah! She's my friend. She *let* me. I am good! I am! I did what I was told! I waited and waited and waited – and Gus never came...' She lost interest in the sandals, stared down at her lap. A slow tear rolled down her cheek and dropped on to her dress, spreading into a stain. Then another. 'You've spoilt it now – you've spoilt everything – I hate you!'

The door opened. Nick entered. 'What's up with Sarah? You're not playing that stupid game are you?' he sneered at Laura.

The girl was bent over now. Curling up into a ball, she seemed to shrink,

'Sarah! Sarah?' Laura leant over her, shaking her.

The girl's shoulders heaved. She started to gag.

'Watch out!' Nick cried. 'I think she's gonna throw up!'

'Quick!' shouted Laura.

Between them they rushed her to the bathroom. They held her over the new gleaming white toilet. Just in time. Fragments of chicken, potatoes, peas and ice-cream splattered into the bowl.

'That's christened it,' said Nick. 'I name this toilet the HMS *Throw-up*. Serve you right, Sarah. For being such a little piggy.'

'Sarah?' said Laura peering anxiously into her face.

'It wasn't me. It must have been Sadie,' moaned Sarah.

Chapter Thirteen

More unusually, some ghosts may display strong personalities, just as in life.

THE HANDBOOK OF HAUNTINGS

Sarah was put to bed. She groaned and moaned for a while then fell asleep.

'Who's been fiddling with my stuff?' demanded Nick in a hoarse whisper. He was searching his chair for his Walkman. 'What?' He shook it. Stared at it. He pressed the rewind button. Then the eject button. He tugged out the cassette. The tape hanging from it looked like crazy brown knitting. 'I don't believe this. You've been mucking around with this!' He threw it at Laura. 'Well – you're going to have to buy me a new one!' he croaked.

'And what's this?' He pulled out Laura's notepad from under his duvet. He flicked through it. He screwed up his face at her. 'That just about does it! You've been using my pen! On your stupid games. You are one sad case, Laura. Right – where is my pen?'

Nick searched his chair, under his cover, then crouched to look under his bed. He stood up slowly. Holding the pen before him. Like it was something sacred that had been defiled. It was his big fat pen with twelve different colours. That a girl called Jasmine had given him on the last day of term.

Laura said nothing. What could she say? It was all so trivial anyway. She watched Nick, wondering what else he would find. She knew it was nothing to do with her. But also that there was little to be gained in telling him this. Or arguing with him. She had to stay calm if she was going to play against Sadie and her games. And try, at some stage, to get through to Nick about what was going on – to get him on her side, if that was remotely possible.

'You're a pain! Know that! A pain in the bum!' he mouthed at her.

He tested out his pen. 'Look – it's broken. The spring's broken!'

In other circumstances it would have been funny. Nick couldn't shout. Their mother had warned them not to disturb Sarah. He tossed the pad and pen at her.

Laura picked up the pad and flicked through it. Page after page, in neat looping writing the word *Sadie*. In twelve different colours.

'I'm very sorry about your pen, Nick,' she said to the pad. 'But I didn't take it. Or use it. That's all I'm going to say. Good night.'

Laura's quiet, impassive manner puzzled Nick. He stared at her warily. Spreading his arms in a theatrical shrug, he fell into bed.

What a very long and very strange day this had been. Exhausted, drained, but relieved that Sarah was back, Laura slid into sleep.

*

Sarah was tetchy next morning.

'My tummy's full of worms,' she complained.

'Well, I'm not surprised,' said Mr Logan.

'Little Miss Greedy,' Nick added.

Sarah frowned from one to the other and then at Laura. Laura tried to shape an expression which said, 'I'll tell you later – when I get the chance.' Sarah gave a martyred sigh, pushed away her uneaten bowl of Rice Crispies and slid off her chair.

What did Sarah remember about last night? Laura wondered. But she did not get the chance to ask Sarah that morning. Their mother announced that she was taking all three of them into Bath for school uniforms. It was a miserable, grey day. It took them half an hour to park. They tramped from shop to shop. By the time they returned home to Hillview House, all were moody. Nick through boredom, Laura preoccupied with thoughts of Sadie and Sarah. Their mother became irritable with their lack of enthusiasm and co-operation. Sarah was subdued, but still insisted on wearing home her new shoes and school sweatshirt.

There were no angry gusts from Sadie waiting to greet them. Mrs White was dozing on the kitchen table. Nick went straight out. Laura beckoned Sarah into the sitting room and shut the door. At last she'd got her on her own.

'Sarah – what do you remember about dinner yesterday?'

Sarah frowned, then shrugged.

'Do you remember eating all that food and ice cream?'

Sarah shook her head.

'What *do* you remember, Sarah?'

'Horrible tummy ache. Yukky sick.'

Laura chewed her thumbnail while she had a think. 'OK, tell me what happened after I left you with Sadie.'

'We played weddings.'

'Then?'

'She got sad again.'

'Yeah? Go on.'

'I was eating my Smarties and she wanted some. She's never had Smarties. Never ever. Then I put on my bridesmaid's dress to show her. Then she got really sad. 'Cos she couldn't dress up. She tried, but it just sort of fell off her. I was very sorry for her. 'Cos I think she might be a ghost after all. Even though she's real. So she said we could have a game when she pretended to be me. And if she pretended hard enough she could be me for a little while. And see what it was like. So she could wear my dress and sandals. And she sort of walked into me. It didn't hurt. Till I had tummy ache. And was sick. And all my things were on the floor. And all my Smarties were gone.'

'Don't you remember anything else?'

'It made me go all cold. Then sleepy. Then I woke up.'

'She came down and pretended to be you,' Laura told her. 'Everyone thought she was you. Except me. But she fooled everyone else. And she wouldn't stop eating. You should have seen her. Finished everything off. And danced around in your dress and sandals. No wonder you felt sick. But she took off then. Left you to have the tummy ache.'

Sarah listened wide eyed as Laura retold the whole

142

episode. 'Perhaps she couldn't help it,' she said. 'She must have been very hungry.'

'But it could be – it could be dangerous, Sarah. And she was still trying to wind me up. And enjoying it. It's all just a game to her.' Laura got up and crouched down before Sarah. 'Listen, Sarah. You must *not* let Sadie do this again. Ever. If she asks again – tell her No. Do you understand, Sarah? What if...' Laura hesitated. Her head was full of what-ifs. What if Sadie didn't give Sarah back next time? What if Sarah couldn't get back again? And other what-ifs too terrible to think about. They scared her. But she didn't want to frighten Sarah.

'Just don't let her do it again. Promise?'

Sarah nodded.

'What about telling Mum and Dad, Sarah? You know they won't believe me. *Please,* Sarah – tell Mum and Dad.'

'But she's my best friend. And I promised. And then perhaps she'll go away – and I don't want her to go away. I like her – she makes me laugh and she's good at making up games.'

Too good, thought Laura.

'Anyway, when I told Daddy that Sadie made me play noughts and crosses with the paint, Daddy said I was a fibber. He'll get cross again. And he'll get cross with you too.'

Laura knew Sarah was right. Anything Sarah said would only rebound on her. They wouldn't believe a word of it and she'd be held responsible. Sadie had made sure of that yesterday with her, *she goes on and on about how Sadie's a ghost.*

143

'Laura! Sarah!' The door opened. 'Who's responsible for this?' demanded their mother angrily. She held up a perfume bottle. 'Do you realise how much this stuff costs? Half of it gone! It's ruined the top of my dressing table! And my jewellery box tipped out and earrings and things all over the place! There's an earring missing too! One of my silver and turquoise ones – I can't find it anywhere!'

Sarah looked at Laura. And Laura looked at Sarah.

'How dare you!' their mother cried. 'Laura! Sarah! Come on. I want an answer!'

'P'raps it was me, Mummy,' said Sarah, looking at Laura. 'P'raps I was just looking and Mrs White jumped up and knocked it all over. And p'raps I was too scared to tell you.'

'Come on – we're going out,' said Laura afterwards.

'No sweeties for two weeks,' sighed Sarah.

'We'll take a picnic.'

'I don't 'spect she did it on purpose. I 'spect she was bored,' said Sarah.

'What do you want to drink? Orange or cola?' asked Laura peering into the fridge.

'I don't want to go on a picnic. Sadie might want to play. I 'spect she called for me this morning when we were out. Do you like my picture? It's me in my new uniform.'

'It's brilliant this place – it's got a stream,' Laura continued. 'You'll really like it. What do you want in your sandwiches, then? Tell you what – but this is a secret – how about we buy some sweeties on the way back?'

After twenty minutes of staring out of the window, Sarah sighed and said, 'All right.'

By the time they'd reached the stream, there was a cold wind. The grass was wet. The sky overcast and threatening to rain.

It's worth it, thought Laura. If I can keep Sarah out of Sadie's way for a bit.

'Good this, isn't it?' said Laura as she huddled into her jumper. Her crisp bag scuttled as the wind took it. She raced after it. 'How about a paddle after?' she munched.

Sarah, almost invisible inside the hood of her jacket, shivered. Laura managed to extend the outing by taking Sarah the long way back, along the stream. By the time they reached the shops, cold rain was driving into their faces. On the way back, Laura stopped suddenly at the corner of Church Lane. It ran behind the church and then became Church Drive, the beginning of the estate of new houses, backing on to Hillview House. Laura took Sarah's hand and they turned into Church Drive. A wet squall slapped their faces.

'Where are we going now?' complained Sarah. 'I want to go home!'

'In a minute – I just want to see something.'

Laura stopped again. Behind the new houses, she could just make out the roof of Hillview House and the branches of their big tree.

'Come on!' whined Sarah, tugging at Laura's hand. 'I want to go!'

They trudged back, Laura absorbed in thought. Those

houses must be where our garden was once, she decided. In Sadie and Gus's time the garden was longer. It had a wall and a gate. Now there's only a fence. No stables any more. But I'm sure that's the way Gus went. The railway must have run further back somewhere. By the time they reached home they were wet and miserable.

Laura spent the remainder of the day in restless anxiety. Watching Sarah for signs of Sadie. But she knew she couldn't watch all the time. And what could she do, anyway, to prevent Sadie doing what she wanted?

'What would you like to do on Friday, Laura?' her mother asked later.

'Friday?' frowned Laura.

'Your birthday – you can't have forgotten.'

Laura answered with an indifferent shrug.

'What d'you want then?' asked Nick. 'Anything you like. As long as it's not more than fifty pee.'

'I'm not bothered,' she said.

'Suit yourself,' said Nick.

Laura felt her mother's eyes rest on her, then a hand on her shoulder.

'Come on – cheer up, love. Think about what you'd like to do and let us know, OK?'

That evening, while they were watching television, the phone rang. Nick called from the kitchen, 'Laura! It's Natalie!' She got up, put her head round the kitchen door and whispered, 'Nick, can you do me a big favour? Tell Nat I'm out or something.'

Nick rolled his eyes.

'Please, Nick.'

He gave a shrug that said, 'if that's what you want – but don't blame me.'

'Er, Nat,' he said, 'She's not feeling very well. Gone all weird. Can't speak. So you know how weird she must be. Yeah. Right. OK.'

He returned the phone to its hook. 'She says she only had one mingy letter. And she's going on holiday for a week. OK?'

'Where's she going?' Laura called after him.

'How do I know?'

Laura sat at the table, doodling on the newspaper, adding plaits and bows to all the heads, wishing she'd talked to Natalie after all, feeling very sorry for herself. Sarah came in fresh from her bath, smelling of talcum and in her nightshirt, to fetch Prudence from the table. Laura went up to look for her letter. It had gone. Only pages of *Sadie*, written in twelve different colours. A chill shivered through her. She hurried down to the kitchen, relieved to see Mrs White licking herself on the boiler. She found a pen and started again.

Dear Nat,
I really really miss you. Sorry I havn't written or phoned. Can't explain here. Its too complicated. Mum says you can come and stay at the end of the holidays. I'll have my own room by then. I've got so much to tell you. You better believe it. No one else does. Please, please.

*

147

If there was one person in the world that Laura wanted to talk to, it was Natalie. Not to natter about sunglasses and haircuts. But to sit down with her and tell her everything. Not on the phone. She'd tried that before. And not with people coming and going. Not with the chance of Sadie listening in. Not with Mum or Dad saying, 'Come on – you've been nattering for fifteen minutes.' And not now, she suddenly realised, when she felt hurt and angry. Angry with Nat for getting on without her. For making new friends. Anyway, it wouldn't even reach her, would it? She'd be on holiday. She felt abandoned. By everyone. She ripped it from the pad and shredded it.

'I want a story, Mummy,' said Sarah, skipping in with Prudence.

Mrs Logan rummaged among the books in one of the cardboard boxes. 'Which one tonight then, Sarah?'

'I'm Sadie tonight, Mummy.'

Laura's head jerked up.

Sadie gave her a dismissive look. She sat on top of the bed waggling and pointing her feet in Sarah's fluffy penguin slippers. She smoothed her Minnie Mouse nightshirt over her knees then slid under the cover. She patted her pillow, made herself comfortable, then switched the bedside light on and off several times. She peered under the cover at her slippers again.

'How about *The Tiger Who Came to Tea*, then? You like that one, don't you?' said Mrs Logan, sitting on the edge of Sarah's bed and cuddling up to the girl.

'Once there was a little girl called Sophie...'

'Mummy?'

'Mmm?'

'Can you tell Laura to go away, please? She keeps staring at me. And she talks too much. It keeps me awake. And tell her not to tell me any more ghost stories.'

Chapter Fourteen

Ghosts are impossible to pin down. They can suddenly materialise or disappear without warning.
THE HANDBOOK OF HAUNTINGS

Laura waited. When she heard her mother come down, she crept back upstairs. Sadie, busily rummaging through the shelves of Sarah's toys, ignored her. She'd been busy. Dolls, toys and games were spread about. She was riffling through them, moving from one thing to another. Like a child deprived of toys who'd just been let loose in a toyshop. She was examining Sarah's musical box now. As she lifted the lid the ballerina popped up and began to twirl to the tinny tune of 'Twinkle Twinkle Little Star'. She abandoned that and reached for the toy stethoscope. She listened, fascinated, to her own heartbeat. Laura noticed there was chocolate round her mouth. A Curly Wurly wrapper lay on the floor. The one Laura had bought for Sarah that afternoon. Sadie was working her way feverishly through the toys and games. Now she was examining an old ping pong gun of Nick's, staring at it, puzzled, then jumped and laughed when she pulled the trigger and a ball shot across the room. She smiled, aimed at Laura and fired, yelling with delight as Laura dodged.

'I've told you before, Sadie – this is wicked! Give Sarah back!'

'Oh, look what I've found,' said Sadie, opening the drawer of Nick's bedside chest.

Laura folded her arms and glared at her. Then went to find Nick. He was giving King Kong a walk along the draining board.

'I just want you to know, Nick, that someone is going through all your cupboards and your stuff. It's nothing to do with me right? I don't want anyone blaming me.'

'Who? Sarah? Well just tell her to pack it in, will you?' he said.

'I have. It didn't make any difference. Don't say I didn't warn you.'

Nick returned King Kong to the cage and, with a suspicious look, followed Laura upstairs. Sadie was fiddling with his camera now.

'Oi – what d'you think you're doing?' he demanded. He snatched it from her and examined it. Then his attention was caught by the open drawer of his bedside chest. 'What?' he cried.

Sadie had found the remains of his Easter egg. He'd been trying to break his record for making one last a year. He only allowed himself occasional tiny nibbles. There was nothing left to nibble now. Just a few tiny crumbs on the crumpled foil inside the open drawer next to his socks. He looked at Sadie, then his drawer, his camera, then at Sadie again. Then he exploded.

'Who do you think you are?' he yelled. 'Who said you could help yourself to any of it! And this is not a toy,

Sarah!' He waved his camera at her. 'Mum! Dad!' he yelled. And went to register a complaint.

By the time their father appeared, Sadie was feigning sleep. She complained that Laura had woken her up and she'd only been looking and was tired and they were keeping her awake. And that Laura must have eaten the chocolate. So Nick loudly accused Laura of causing trouble, while Sadie yawned and sighed about all the noise.

'Both of you – out!' Mr Logan ordered Laura and Nick. 'You're keeping Sarah awake!'

The little girl was still awake when Laura went up, singing a song to herself.

Sadie, beautiful Sadie,
You're the only g-g-g-girl that I adore...

Nick was already in bed, humming tunelessly to his Walkman. 'I'm going to have a padlock on my door,' he announced loudly.

At last it became quiet. The luminous red dots of Nick's clock pricked the semi-darkness. Laura got out of bed. Sadie – or Sarah – appeared to be asleep. She returned to bed, waiting stiffly in the dark, glancing occasionally at Sarah's bed, thinking and listening to the sound of her parents coming and going and the bathroom door opening and shutting. After what seemed ages, the landing light went out. Laura was determined to stay awake, but drowsiness crept up on her. She woke with a start, to the sound of the door swishing. In the darkness, she could just make out a small figure crossing the room, then slide into Sarah's bed. A car passed, its headlights leaking through the flimsy curtains and sliding across the walls. Caught in its yellow beam, a small pale, face flickered against the darkness above Sarah's bed. A glimpse so brief that Laura could not be certain whether she had imagined or seen it. Wide awake now, rigid with tension, she stared. She heard a long, slow sigh. Then it was dark again. She leapt up and rushed to Sarah's bed.

'Sadie?' No answer. 'Sarah – Sarah – wake up...' She shook her gently. Squinted in the dark at her face. She could smell something sweet. She shook her again. 'Wake up, Sarah!'

'What? What d'you want?' Sarah responded sleepily. She rubbed her eyes.

'You forgot Prudence,' whispered Laura, picking the pig up from the floor. 'Go back to sleep, Sarah.'

'Don't look at *me*,' said Laura quietly. 'If it was me – which it wasn't – I wouldn't have made it so obvious, would I?'

She'd just walked into the kitchen for breakfast. On the table stood open jars – of chocolate spread, golden syrup, jam, peanut butter... Sticky spoons lay everywhere. The biscuit tin lay on its side in a scattering of crumbs. The worktop was littered with the remains of a banana, an apple and other snacks. Nick chewed on his muesli, studying Laura with curiosity.

'Just look at the mess,' snapped Mrs Logan, waving an arm around the kitchen. 'Nick says it's nothing to do with him – so who was it?'

'And whoever it was left the fridge open,' said their father, looking at Laura. 'Food doesn't grow on trees, you know.'

Nick spluttered a mouthful of muesli over the table.

'And if this is meant to be a joke – it's not very funny,' added Mr Logan.

'I agree with you,' said Laura, pouring some orange juice.

'Well, *someone's* been midnight feasting, and if it wasn't Nick and it wasn't you, who was it?' said their mother again.

They all turned to look at Sarah as she walked in, trailing Prudence.

'Mmmm,' said Nick. 'Somehow I don't think we're going to need Inspector Morse to solve this one.'

'What's the matter?' said Sarah.

Her face was smeared with chocolate. There was a small jammy handprint on her nightshirt. Despite this, and the fact she didn't want breakfast because she felt too full up, she protested her innocence.

'P'raps it was Sadie,' she added.

'No, Sarah – we both know it couldn't have been Sadie, don't we?' said their father impatiently. 'You haven't forgotten what I said the other day? About fibbing?'

'P'raps it *was* me, then,' said Sarah, looking down at her nightshirt, then at Laura.

Mrs Logan eyed Laura and Nick. 'You two ought to be ashamed of yourselves – letting Sarah take all the blame!

You can take those innocent expressions of your faces right now!'

'Don't look at me!' cried Nick. 'I reckon Laura knows more about this than she's letting on.'

'Clear it up,' said Mrs Logan. 'All three of you.'

'That's not fair!' protested Nick.

'I can't remember,' said Sarah when Laura asked what had happened.

'Did you see Sadie?'

Sarah shook her head. Laura's anxiety increased. Sadie was slipping in and taking over without Sarah even knowing it. She stayed close to Sarah. Throughout the day Sarah had been singing snatches of the song she'd sung the night before.

Sadie, beautiful Sadie!
You're the only g-g-g-girl that I adore!
When the m-m-m-moon shines
Over the cow shed
I'll be waiting at the k-k-k-kitchen door!

'Well! Wherever did you learn that?' Mrs Logan asked.

'I don't know,' she shrugged. 'It just came into my head.'

'Isn't it meant to be Katie? Not Sadie. It goes "Katie, beautiful Katie," doesn't it?' said their mother later.

'Must have picked it up from all that telly-watching,' said Nick.

*

They were playing picture consequences. Sarah had just opened her strip of paper. She blinked several times, as if trying to focus, then lifted her head and stared out of the window.

'Rain,' she said. 'I want to feel the rain.'

And Laura knew that Sadie had taken over again. While they were playing she had silently slipped in. Just as she must have done the evening before. Sadie was already heading for the back door. Laura jumped up and followed, watched her stand with her face upturned to the soft drizzle. Sadie started to wade slowly through the long wet grass, arms outstretched, bending to trail her hands in it. Then she began to spin. Round and round she spun till she was dizzy. She stopped, laughing as she staggered to gain her balance, then ran towards the big tree, paused for a second and started to climb.

'Wait!' Laura called.

Sadie ignored her, working her way up. Now she was balancing on a thin branch, holding on to the trunk. Laura climbed after her, Sadie laughing as she slipped out of reach.

'That's far enough,' Laura called. 'Stop!'

She wondered what to do next. The branch on which Sadie was standing didn't look as if it would take her weight. Laura manoeuvred herself round and grabbed for Sadie's ankle

'Let go!' ordered Sadie. 'If you do that again – I'll jump.' She smiled.

Laura looked down. They were higher than she had thought. Sadie reached forward to get a grasp on an overhanging branch, missed and teetered dangerously before regaining her balance and a hold of the trunk again. Laura could hardly bear to look.

'Look – no hands!' laughed Sadie, letting go. 'It's all right – don't worry. I've done this lots of times before, you know. Whoops! Anyway – *I* can't get hurt.' She swayed deliberately, eyeing Laura's helplessness. Then, laughing, she reached for the trunk and leant against it. 'See?' she called. She peered down and probed with her foot. 'Oh dear,' she said. 'I think it's rather more difficult coming down than going up.'

The thought that Sadie might suddenly leave occurred to Laura. She could picture Sarah waking – drowsy, confused...

'Sit down!' she shouted. 'Hold on to the trunk and see if you can sit down!'

Sadie laughed at her and continued to climb. She disappeared out of sight into a mass of leaves.

Laura raced back to the house, her head full of images of Sarah hurtling downwards through the branches.

Sadie sat, watching calmly from the top of the tree as Mr and Mrs Logan rushed about, fetching the ladder, calling up frantically, 'Stay still, Sarah! Don't move!'

Her last words before departing, as Mr Logan reached up for her were, 'Laura bet me fifty pee I couldn't do it, Daddy. I'm clever aren't I?'

'Are you out of your mind, Laura! I'm worried about you! Seriously worried!' he stormed.

Sarah sat on her mother's lap, wrapped in a towel. She was pale and droopy.

'It wasn't really Laura's fault,' she said listlessly. 'P'raps it wasn't her idea – I can't remember. P'raps it was Sadie made me go up the tree and...'

'That's enough! See, Laura! See what you've put into her head! I never want to hear the word 'Sadie' mentioned again in this house. Never! And that goes for you too, Sarah. Do I make myself clear?' said their father.

Nick heard the story later. 'You've really got them going,' he grinned.

'Says the person who got caught up the tree by his knickers,' Laura sighed, staring out of the window.

'No – I mean all that Sadie stuff. And how you've been feeding it to Sarah. I heard Mum say she might speak to the doctor. They think you need help.'

Laura turned slowly.

'They're right,' she sighed. 'But not that sort.'

'You *are* nuts.'

'If you say so, dear brother.'

'You'll just make things worse for yourself.'

'You're probably right.'

Nick was flummoxed by this recent change in Laura's manner. He could usually arouse her to loud fury. He tried provoking her again.

'It won't work you know. Pretending to be bonkers won't make them move back. You're going to have to get used to it here.'

'Thanks for the advice, Nick.'

Laura wandered downstairs. Sarah had gone out with her mother. Her father was putting up shelves in the kitchen. Among some letters lying on the mat in the hallway, she spotted several birthday cards. She recognised her grandmother's handwriting. She always sent hers a day early. But what caught her attention was the blue Bonusprint envelope. Photos, Laura thought. Nick's photos. The ones I took of him. She had almost forgotten them.

She snatched up the package, ran up to the bathroom and locked the door. She wanted the first look. She sat there looking down at the blue envelope. In the light of what had happened since, her eagerness to see inside seemed silly. But it would take her mind off things. She needed the reassurance of something normal. She found the nail scissors and carefully cut the package open. She withdrew the envelope, lifted the flap, tugged out the wodge of photos.

The first one was of her mother. Her face reflected by a mirror. Like twin faces looking away. It was a good photo. She flicked through them. His judo club crowd. Their old house. Nick's room. His friends. Her own crossed-eyed face in the shed window. The dead rat in the cellar. Herself asleep, her thumb in her mouth. She tore it up and the shed one too. Several of the back of the house and the garden. And yes... Laura smiled. Nick caught up the tree. Dad with the ladder and Nick looking down. Dad up the ladder... A sudden thought made Laura stop. She glanced over her shoulder. Sadie might be watching. Stuffing the photos down her shirt she went to search for Mrs White. She found her on the kitchen table, carried her back, locked the door and returned to the photos.

Nick almost upside down, his shorts slipping. And, yes, Nick's bottom.

Laura held this one up close. She stared hard. 'Yes,' she said quietly, staring down at it. 'Oh yes.'

She grabbed the next photo, then the next. She ran through them again. And again. 'Yes, oh yes, oh yes.'

Laura ran to her bed and slid the packet under the mattress as far as her arm would reach. Then she fetched her pen and pad and sat down. After much careful thought she wrote a letter. She read it through twice. Folding it, she slipped it into an envelope, sealed it and wrote something on the envelope. She slid it deep into her jeans pocket.

'Do you want a present for your birthday or not?' said Nick when he came in. 'I keep asking. You shouldn't have left it so late.'

She was watching television with Sarah. Nick looked at his watch.

'Quick – the shops close in half an hour. It'll have to be something that I can get at the Spar. Or the newsagent's.'

'Don't worry,' said Laura. 'I know what I want.'

'Go on, then.'

'I'll tell you in the morning. After breakfast.'

'That'll be too late.'

'No it won't. I want it on my birthday.'

'But I might not have what you want.'

'Don't worry. You have.'

'It's not my camera is it? You're not having that.'

'No. Don't worry – and it won't cost a penny. You won't even miss it.'

Chapter Fifteen

The very nature of ghosts makes it
almost impossible to prove their existence.
THE HANDBOOK OF HAUNTINGS

The strained mood from yesterday's events remained next morning.

'Thanks, Mum, thanks, Dad.' Laura tried to sound cheerful as she opened her presents: a new shirt and a bag from her parents. From Sarah a bottle of bubble bath. There were some more cards and parcels to open.

'Where's your present, Nick?' asked their mother.

'It's a surprise,' said Nick. ('To me anyway,' he said under his breath.)

'Come on then,' Laura said when they were on their own. 'Surprise time – let's go. Sarah – you can come with us.'

'What? Where are we going?' said Nick.

'Out.'

'What are we doing here?' Nick asked. They had reached the little park. Apart from a dog sniffing at a tree it was empty.

'Look, Sarah – you've got it all to yourself. Swings, slide, rocking horse – all yours,' said Laura.

Sarah sighed and wandered off. Laura sat on the bench

and watched Sarah sit on one of the swings, hooking her arms round the chains with Prudence on her lap, staring at the ground, trailing her feet listlessly.

'Well?' Nick shrugged.

Laura tugged the letter from her jeans and held it out to him.

'What's this?' he said.

'Don't open it. Read the envelope first. Then give me your answer. Promise.'

'Curiouser and curiouser,' Nick grinned. 'OK.' He looked down and read:

> *BEFORE OPENING THIS ENVELOPE YOU MUST AGREE TO THESE CONDITIONS.*
> 1. *I will listen to everything you tell me.*
> 2. *I will not interrupt, get angry, or make faces.*
> 3. *I PROMISE FAITHFULY this will remain a secret between us unless Laura decides otherwise.*
>
> *SIGNED...*
> *DATE..*

'You've spelt faithfully wrong,' Nick said.

'Do you agree? Yes or no?'

Nick rubbed his nose. 'You said it won't cost anything?'

'Not a penny.'

'Mmmm – OK.'

'All the conditions – you promise?'

'Cross my eyes and let the giant lobsters loose in my underpants if I lie.'

'This is serious Nick.' Laura held out a pen. 'Sign.'

Nick signed with a flourish, slit the envelope with his finger, pulled out the paper and unfolded it.

'Is that all?' he said, staring at the piece of paper.

Laura had written: *I WANT THIRTY MINUTES OF YOUR TIME.*

'Don't forget the conditions,' said Laura. She focused on her hands, took a deep breath and began.

'Listen. I *know* – for certain – that Sadie was a real child. A girl. She lived in our house. And she died. And she is now a ghost-child...'

Nick opened his mouth, snorted a dismissive laugh and shook his head.

'I knew you wouldn't keep your promise,' Laura hissed. She snatched the envelope and shook it at him. 'No interruptions! No stupid faces! Thirty minutes! You promised. There's no going back on a promise!'

'OK, OK. Calm down. Go on. I'll do my best not to laugh.'

Laura closed her eyes to shut out his grinning face and took another deep breath.

'The reason she died is something to do with Gus. Gus left her somewhere. She waited, but Gus didn't go back for her. This is what Sarah says Sadie told her. And what Sarah told me.'

A flicker of derision crossed Nick's face.

'I think Sarah might be psychic or something. She can see her and hear her and she plays with her. At first I wasn't really sure, but if you'd watched and listened to Sarah playing with Sadie like I have, and seen the things I have,

165

you'd be as certain as I am. And Mrs White knows. She always knows when Sadie's there. Sadie gives her the creeps – she hisses, backs off and scoots – like when she brought in the guinea pig? Sadie wants Sarah all to herself. She's lonely...'

Nick rolled his eyes and sighed.

'...Sadie doesn't like me...'

Nick nodded with understanding.

Laura ignored him, kept her eyes on the ground and concentrated on what she was saying.

'She knows I know – but she doesn't want anyone interfering. For a while she made Sarah pretend she wasn't there, made her say that it was all pretend. She always behaves herself in front of Mum and Dad and you – except to play tricks on me. The flying potato was just one of them. To Sarah she's just funny. Most of the time. And it was Sadie who let out your insects – not me.'

Nick struggled to keep still.

'I haven't got time to tell you all the stuff that's happened. At first she just seemed harmless. But she's really cunning – gets Sarah doing things she wouldn't normally. Even when she upsets her, she gets round her again. She wants Sarah all to herself – and she loves winding me up – like flicking the telly on and off. Remember?'

Nick looked at his watch.

'And remember that time when the bedroom door was jammed – and all that noise? Well that was Sadie – having an enormous tantrum. She was jealous, see, because Sarah had been out playing with Becky. Remember that day?

After that it got worse – really frightening, Nick. You know that time Sarah was twirling away in her bridesmaid dress? Well – it wasn't Sarah. It was Sadie. Sadie had taken her over – taken over her body. '

Nick snorted a mocking laugh, rolled his eyes and fidgeted on his seat, shaking his head. He was finding it hard not to interrupt.

'Since then she's been doing it more and more. And Sarah can't stop her. It's wearing her out. Just look at her, Nick.' Laura pointed to their sister.

Sarah was leaning against a tree now, hugging her pig, watching two boys on the climbing frame.

'Sadie wants to be a little girl again, Nick. Dressing up and eating nice food. Being cuddled by Mum. All the sorts of things she hasn't done for years and years. She likes it so much, she can't stop. She's taking control of Sarah, Nick. And Sarah can't stop her – she doesn't even know when it's happening. It's not a joke. I'm not crazy. Remember the way she was eating all that food? That was Sadie. But it was Sarah who was sick. The midnight feast in the kitchen? That was Sadie too. Sarah doesn't remember any of it. And yesterday up the tree – that was Sadie again. Just think about it, about what might have happened if she'd fallen. She's not harmless, Nick. She's *dangerous*. And she's getting stronger and stronger. All the time Sarah is in that house she's in danger, Nick.'

Nick had an expression of irritation now. He leant forward and buried his face in his hands, shaking his head.

'Nick! Listen! This is not funny! You're going to look a right idiot when you realise that!'

She was furious with his face-pulling and joking. She wanted to hit him, but she made herself calm down.

'You've cheated me of at least five minutes. I'm stopping till you play by the conditions. We can sit here all day – I don't care.'

'OK,' he sighed. Laura realised he wasn't mocking her now. He was looking at her strangely, warily, a little frightened even. Not as if he *believed* her. But as if he was beginning to wonder whether she was suffering from mental delusions.

'Right, that's roughly the story so far,' she continued. 'Now the evidence. Remember the time we went out for a pizza? When you were in the bathroom you powdered your knees with Mum's talc – to save having to wash. How do I know? Sadie was in there with you. She told Sarah. Sarah told me.'

Nick frowned and opened his mouth.

'No interruptions, Nick. I also know that you accidentally trod on one of your stick insects. You flushed it down the sink – but it stuck and you had to pick it out of the plug. You threw it at Shane, didn't you? No one but you could know that. We were all out that day. Except Sadie – who told Sarah, who told me.'

Nick was looking confused now and bursting now to say something.

'I've left a lot out,' she said. 'But I think you still don't believe a thing I've told you. So I want to show you something.'

From the inside of her jacket, she took out the Bonusprint envelope. As she pulled out the photos Nick glared and tried to grab them.

'Patience, Nick. You can have them in a minute. Remember this?'

She passed the first shot of him up the tree. 'And this – and this – and this...'

Nick fidgeted with annoyance and glared as he shuffled through them.

'Apart from knowing what it feels like to be made to look stupid, and before you chuck them, just look there. You could almost miss her.' She pointed at a branch in the photo. Nick glanced briefly, then stared more intently. 'And this one. And these. Look very carefully, Nick, there – and there.'

Laura passed them all over. Nick shook his head. His jaw bounced up and down like a yo-yo. He ran his hand through his hair. Looked again. Went through each photo carefully. In each one was the faintest impression of a young girl. At first glance she could be missed. At the second explained away by the pattern of leaves, the cast of a shadow or sunlight. But with the photos side by side the impression of a girl with long plaits and bows emerged. Sitting on a branch, legs dangling feet in black shoes, mostly looking across at Nick but in one looking straight at the camera. He stared and blinked.

'All right – you can speak now,' Laura told him.

Nick's mouth worked silently for a second or two. 'It's not possible – it's faked – you fixed a double exposure, or something like that,' he stammered.

'OK – here's the one *you* took of the garden.' She passed it across.

'Look at the bush there, see? I couldn't see her at first.

169

She blends into the leaves. See? Standing looking at you, with her arms folded.'

Nick slumped back and puffed out a long slow breath.

'I've still got ten minutes, Nick.'

Laura turned to Sarah climbing down from the rocking horse. 'Sarah – come here a minute!' she called.

She lifted Sarah on to her lap, took the photos from Nick and showed Sarah one of them. 'Who's this, Sarah – see there?'

'It's Sadie – Sadie up the tree. I told you – she saw you take Nick's camera.'

'Go on, Nick. Ask her. Ask her anything you like. I've got seven minutes left.'

Nick reached out for the photos. He hunched over them, frowning. Laura waited, her body stiff with tension.

'Bloody hell,' he breathed slowly.

Laura didn't know whether to laugh or cry. She didn't want to hit him any more.

'Better tell me again – all of it,' he said, staring down at the photos. 'I wasn't really paying attention.'

'Can we go home now?' Sarah sighed, after Nick had interrogated her.

'What?' said Nick. 'Oh yeah – just a few more minutes, eh?'

He looked at Laura, spread out his hands palms up in a lengthy shrug. Then slowly released it. She could read his shrugs like a book. It was a shrug of defeat. It was the best present she could have had.

'What sort of ghost is she!' he spluttered. 'Watching me in the bog! Some sort of bathroom pervert is she? You mean she could have been watching me? All the time?'

'There's loads I haven't told you,' said Laura as they set off home. 'Like my dreams – I've been having them since we moved here. About Gus – as if I *am* Gus. And it's not my imagination – I can prove it...' It all spilled out.

'Hang about,' said Nick. 'I can't take all of this in.' He stopped on the corner by the church. 'We've got to tell Mum and Dad,' he said.

'That's what I've been trying to do. For weeks, Nick. I just needed someone to take me seriously. But I know Dad'll probably self-destruct if *I* mention the word Sadie again. They'll listen to you Nick. Even *they* can't ignore the photos. You wouldn't have believed me, would you? Not without them?'

'I don't really believe it now. I've got to accept it – but...' His voice trailed off as he shuffled through the photos again. 'OK. I'll talk to them. It won't be easy. And I'm not sure I'm quite convinced about Sarah being taken over – what's it called? 'Possession' – that's it. You sure you aren't imagining that bit? I mean... OK, OK. Calm down.'

Chapter Sixteen

Science tells us that ghosts do not exist.
Experience tells us otherwise.
THE HANDBOOK OF HAUNTINGS

'We need to pick the right moment,' said Nick as they reached the gate.

The back door was locked. They went round to the front and pressed the bell. Mr Samson opened the door.

'Your mum and dad've gone to pick up some tiles – asked me to hold the fort, like. I'm upstairs if you need me – doing their en suite.'

'We ought to take it in turns to keep watch,' Laura whispered as she made some coffee, signalling with her eyes towards Sarah. She was flopped over the table, head on her arms, tracing patterns with a finger on to the wood. 'This house gives me the creeps,' she said under her breath, 'never knowing when Sadie's going to turn up. Perhaps we ought to go out – it's safer.'

Nick opened the cupboard door and peered at the height chart. 'It's weird. They couldn't have known then, could they? That Sadie only had a little while to live. Makes you think, doesn't it? You never know what's coming. Just as well, I s'pose. Over eighty years she's been dead – most likely Gus is dead too.' He sat down with his mug of coffee, took out the photos and examined them again. Sarah lifted her head and leant over. 'This is not scientifically possible,' he insisted.

'I wish Mum and Dad would come home,' said Laura, biting a fingernail. 'I just want to get it over with. What are you going to say?'

'I'll think of something. They'll have to believe it, won't they? When they see these.'

'Yeah – but what can they do? Even if they believe us?' Laura paced up and down. 'I mean – what can they actually do?'

'I dunno – ask the vicar in or something. Call a ghostbuster. Someone who knows how to get rid of her. Remember that programme on telly? I didn't believe any of that – thought it was rubbish.'

'Oh no – not now,' Laura mumbled, looking towards the window.

'What?'

'Noddy's come to play.'

'Don't be rude about my friend! He puts up with you, doesn't he?'

'How yer doin'?' bobbed Shane as Nick unlocked the door.

Nick launched into how he was a bit busy today and how his mother had all these jobs lined up for him.

'Okey-dokes,' bobbed Shane. 'I only came round to say I can't come round. Got to go and see my grandad, just wondered like, if you wanted to come along. What about later then?'

Nick rubbed the back of his neck, 'Er – dunno – leave it for a bit. I'll come round if I can.'

'Okey-dokes, then.'

Laura dropped into a chair. 'I've got a headache,' she groaned, rubbing her eyes.

'See ya, then,' said Shane, heading for the door.

'Hey – Shane!' called Laura as a thought hit her.

'Yeah?'

'You know the old railway?'

He nodded.

'You know you said it came through the village once...'

'Yeah.'

'You don't know where, do you?'

'Yeah – the other side of the new estate. Part of the embankment's still there. There's a gap between the houses. Can't miss it – there's some steps leadin' up.'

'That's where Gus used to go – the place I dreamt about,' she told Nick when Shane had left. Laura jolted upright. 'Nick! Where's Sarah?'

They looked at one another, then at the open back door, and dashed into the garden.

'Sarah!' Laura called.

'Sshh – listen,' said Nick.

They stood still. A long way off they could hear a small voice singing, '*Sadie, beautiful Sadie...*' They peered down the garden. Then Laura turned and looked up. Her stomach lurched. She heard Nick's sharp intake of breath.

High above them, dangling her legs, Sarah sat on the narrow ledge of one of the attic windows. She was staring

175

ahead. Staring into the distance beyond the garden and the roofs, singing her song. But with long, slow words, stretching out the tune. A sad, empty, lonely song that sent a cold shiver through Laura. For a fraction of a second, though it seemed longer, they both froze. Both thinking the same thing. One slip, one clumsy movement and she would plunge down to the paving stones below.

'Oh no,' Laura choked. 'It's Sadie, Nick! She's got Sarah again!'

Yet even now, Laura saw a momentary flicker of doubt cross Nick's face. Then, suddenly mobilised, they both turned and raced inside and up the stairs. Panting, they paused outside the door.

'Careful,' panted Laura. 'We've got to be careful. Remember it's Sadie. If she leaves suddenly, Sarah won't know what's happening – or where she is. Don't rush...' She slipped in, Nick behind her. 'Sadie?' Laura said softly.

Sadie continued her slow sad song.

'Please, Sadie, come back in. Please. If – if you fall – you'll get hurt.'

Sadie stopped singing. Slowly she leant forward and peered down. Laura's stomach plunged violently. She glanced at Nick. His face was white.

'You're sad, aren't you?' said Laura. 'Because of what you heard Nick say.'

'*I* can't get hurt. Not any more.' Sadie's voice seem to be shrinking.

Nick frowned. 'But Sarah can. You don't want to hurt Sarah, do you, Sadie. She's your friend.'

Sadie swung her legs.

'Please – please – come inside,' pleaded Laura again. 'If you slip, Sarah will be killed.'

Sadie gave an almost imperceptible shrug. 'Then she'll be the same as me. And we'll be friends for ever and ever.' Her voice had a distant, wishful sound.

Laura felt the sweat break out on her palms. She threw a desperate, helpless look at Nick. His face was damp, his body locked with tension.

'Where are you, Gus?' Sadie chanted, almost to herself. 'I'm waiting. Look – I'm waiting. Just like you made me promise. You mustn't break promises, must you?' she chanted.

Nick took a step forward. Laura shot him a warning look. Then Sadie did something that made Laura gasp and hold her breath.

Sadie stood up and stepped out on to the narrow ledge.

'Sadie...' said Nick. His voice was a croak. 'Look – we can help you, if you come inside. If you hurt Sarah, she won't want to be your friend, will she? Then you'll be all on your own again. You don't want that. Come inside. If you come in, I promise we'll do everything we can to find Gus...'

Sadie lifted her eyes from the ground and looked at them, frowning, as if thinking.

Laura knew she had to keep her attention.

'Tell us, Sadie – was it here? Was this where Gus said to wait – at the window? Did you fall out?'

Slowly, Sadie shook her head. Nick took a step forward. Sadie lifted an arm. Laura stiffened as Sadie pointed out with her hand.

'There,' she pointed.

Their eyes followed the direction of her arm. To the sky. Nick leapt forward and snatched at the girl.

Together they fell.

Chapter Seventeen

*What all psychic experiences have in common, is the way
in which they defy the limits of the real, natural world.*
THE HANDBOOK OF HAUNTINGS

Nick lay on the floor where they had fallen, still clasping
Sarah. Sarah opened her eyes. She was confused and
couldn't remember how she got there, then became quiet
and withdrawn.

Sadie is wearing her out, thought Laura. She's sucking
out all her energy. But Sadie's changed too. Like it's not
enough – taking over Sarah. Like it only reminds her of
what she's lost. And she's tired of it all. And of waiting.
And it's as if she's left traces of herself behind in Sarah.

The three of them sat on the front step, Sarah hugging
Prudence and leaning against Nick.

Laura had found Mrs White and had her on her lap.
'We can't stay here,' she said, rubbing her temples. 'I wish
my head would stop aching. It feels as if something is
pressing down on me. Can't you feel it?'

'It's just the weather,' said Nick, looking up.

The sky was colourless, without brightness now. The air
was still and heavy. He looked at his watch. 'Taking their
time, aren't they?'

'That was a good ploy – what you said about Gus,' said Laura.

Nick kicked at a dandelion sprouting on the path. 'What d'you think she meant – when she pointed at the sky?' he asked. 'It doesn't make any sense.'

Laura shrugged. Then looked up slowly and said, 'Yes it does. She wasn't pointing at the sky – she was pointing to the railway! Where it used to be – where Gus used to go – I told you!'

Laura knelt down in front of Sarah. 'What was it Sadie said, Sarah? She waited and waited – but she got fed up with waiting. So she went to look. But she couldn't find anyone...'

Sarah nodded.

'Listen, Nick. In my dream Gus used to go there – it was a secret – it was like he was meeting someone. There was a sort of den place. Perhaps Sadie followed him – and got lost – and she waited – but something happened...'

Nick looked unconvinced. 'Yeah, but it *was* only a dream – probably triggered by what Shane told us when we were out the other day. All mixed up with your imagination about Gus.'

'Yes – people keep telling me it's all my imagination. Sadie was all my imagination – remember?'

'All right,' Nick shrugged. 'How does it help us – even if it was true?'

'I don't know – but I want to go and look.'

'OK,' he sighed.

*

As the three of them walked, Laura described her dreams to Nick. '...and the garden was longer then. It came right out – there,' she pointed as they turned into Church Drive. 'See where those new houses are? And it had a wall and a gate.'

'Shane said the other side of the estate – we ought to turn left here,' said Nick.

'I'm tired! I want Mummy,' Sarah moaned.

The road curved and wound with numerous turnings.

'Are you sure we're not going back on ourselves?' Laura asked.

Nick frowned. He was carrying Sarah piggy-back now. They reached a cul-de-sac with a circular turning area at the far end.

'It's a dead end,' announced Laura. 'Come on – let's go back.'

'Wait,' called Nick. 'Look.'

He pointed to a post with a small sign. It said 'Footpath and Cycle Path' and pointed to an alley between two houses.

Laura ran down the alley, saw ahead a sloping bank into which were set a flight of wooden steps. She climbed to the top. The embankment stretched in either direction – just as she remembered. But there were no black rails resting on heavy wooden sleepers. No stones and clinker beneath her feet. Just a path and grass. She looked down on to the gardens of the house below her and to Nick with Sarah on his back, reaching the top of the steps.

'See? This is the old railway line. Didn't I tell you? How could I have known that?'

Laura set off along the top, Nick following, calling, 'Hang about – where are we going?'

'I want to see – to see if it's how I remember,' she called back.

'Stop, stop, I want to stop,' Sarah whimpered.

Nick let her get down. He looked at Laura who was well ahead. 'We ought to get back,' he called.

Laura turned away, searching the distance for something she recognised. The chimney, the tower with the wheel, all gone now. The sky had darkened to the colour of tarmac. Everything seemed grey and lifeless, like a black and white photo. At that moment, it all seemed unreal. Her dream had been real, but not this. 'Somewhere out there is Gus's den,' she called, pointing. 'It was in a dip – under some bushes.'

But there were dips and slopes and clumps of trees and bushes as far as the eye could see.

'Take your pick,' said Nick wearily, waving an arm. 'Look – this isn't getting us anywhere. And Sarah's all in. Mum and Dad should be home by now – come on.'

He bent down and heaved Sarah on to his back.

'They're back,' said Nick, seeing their parents' car. Mr Logan was unloading boxes into the hall. 'Let me do this on my own,' Nick muttered.

'Oh – so there you are,' said their mother as they entered the kitchen. 'Look – I couldn't resist this, Laura. An extra birthday present.'

She took a small package from a carrier bag. Inside was an enamelled name plate with 'Laura's Room' on it, beneath a rainbow.

'And what about a Chinese takeaway tonight? And we could get a video if you like?'

'Yeah, great – thanks, Mum,' said Laura with forced enthusiasm.

She glanced at Sarah, sitting at the table, leaning wearily on her arms. Laura threw an urgent look at Nick. He was peering anxiously behind his insect cage, then under newspapers, the bread bin, the chairs – as if he had lost something. He turned to Laura and gave a despairing shrug. He looked panic-stricken.

Mr Samson appeared in the doorway. 'I'll be off for a bite to eat then. Feels like a storm's brewing,' he said to their mother.

Nick headed upstairs and Laura after him, taking Mrs White with her.

'They've gone!' whispered Nick, shutting the door. 'I can't believe it – the photos have vanished!'

'You stupid...' she hissed. 'Why didn't you keep them on you? After all I've told you – oh Nick...'

She was too angry, too upset, to finish. Her head felt as if it was turning to concrete.

'But I hid them! I put them inside my computer mag and slid it behind the insect cage! How can they have gone?' He paced up and down, as if talking to himself.

'She saw you, Nick,' said Laura, sinking on to her bed. 'Sadie saw you – and heard you. That wasn't Sarah sitting at the table – it was Sadie. She heard you say she was dead – that Gus was probably dead too. And she saw the photos. I think that's what upset her. I don't think she understands any of this herself. Let's face it – we don't

183

understand. And she's scared – scared of losing Sarah. There's no telling what she might do next.' She sank her face into her hands. 'What are we going to do, Nick? I don't like leaving Sarah – not even for a minute – especially now.' She stood up.

Nick stared down at the floor, as if in deep thought. 'Look – I'll just try telling them,' he said. 'I'll tell them about the photos – and everything else...'

He stared at the floor for several seconds, then opened the door and left. Laura paced impatiently. Nick returned five minutes later.

'Well?' she demanded.

'I couldn't,' he said, flopping on to his bed and holding his head. 'I just couldn't. It'd have been a waste of time. I got Dad on his own – he was in the garden. But I bottled out. *I* wouldn't believe it – not without the photos. So Dad won't, that's for sure. Not certain I really believe it even now. Keep thinking that any minute I'll wake up.'

'Where's Sarah? Is she all right?' said Laura.

'Yeah – she's with Mum in the kitchen. You're not allowed in. They're making a cake or something. It's a surprise. But I didn't like leaving her.'

'I've been thinking... I might be wrong, but I don't think Sadie will bother her – not straight away. I think it wears her out too. I think she'll wait and see what happens. You could see her thinking when you said you'd try and find Gus. Trouble is, we haven't got a hope. She won't wait for ever. What are we going to do then, Nick?'

'I'm thinking about it,' he said.

They sat there for several minutes. Then Laura said,

184

'I've just remembered – there's something I want to show you.' She got up and opened the cupboard door. 'Look down there – under all your stuff. There's a loose board. Go on – look.'

'Hey, there's something down there,' Nick said reaching in.

'I know,' Laura said as he lifted out the tobacco tin. 'Inside there are two cigarettes and some matches.'

'How did you know they were...' he paused. 'Don't tell me – you dreamt it.'

Laura nodded.

Nick lifted out one of the cigarettes and slowly turned it between his fingers.

'Right – let's think,' he said. 'We've got to be systematic about this. So – what do we know about Sadie? One, she's dead – and she must have died sometime after she was measured – age seven – on the twelfth of January, nineteen twenty-three. Perhaps she doesn't realise she's dead. Perhaps we should tell her.'

'I did – it didn't do any good,' Laura told him.

'OK,' said Nick. 'Two, she lived here once. Three, she's still here. Why?'

'Because Gus told her to wait,' said Laura. 'Because she promised and she's still waiting. That's what she told Sarah. It's as if she can't go – not till Gus comes.'

'Mmmm,' said Nick. 'OK – let's find him. Or at least try and find out if he's dead or alive.'

Laura threw up her hands. 'It's impossible!'

'Not necessarily,' said Nick. 'Perhaps there are people living around here who remember them both. People of

185

their age. Look – Sadie would have been about eighty-seven now – and Gus over ninety.'

'Yeah – but what if we discover Gus is dead – then what?' said Laura.

'One thing at a time,' said Nick, replacing the tin and the floorboard. 'We could ask at the library – about old people's clubs or homes. Come on. We've got to start somewhere.'

'There's only a mobile library,' Laura told him. 'But I can't remember which day – there's a poster in the post office window.'

'Thursdays! Damn!' said Nick.

'What about this?' asked Laura, reading out from another poster in the window. 'Storrington Past – a photographic exhibition by Storrington Historical Society, August the twelfth to the twenty-fourth in the village hall. Entrance free. Any offers of the loan of photographs will be appreciated. Please telephone Mrs Hardcastle...'

Inside the hall, a woman with tightly curled grey hair sat at a green felt card table on which booklets and leaflets were spread out. It was so dark now that all the hall lights were on.

'Excuse me,' said Nick. 'We're trying to find out about our house and who used to live there – it's quite an old house but we don't know where to start.'

'Well, there are the deeds of the house – and various public records you could research,' she smiled. 'We have a leaflet here which might help – thirty pence.' She tapped a pink pile.

'What we really want to know is if they're still alive,' said Laura. 'We found some dates and names on a door. One of them would be about ninety now – his name was Gus something.'

'Is this in Storrington?' she asked.

'Hillview House on Storrington Road,' said Nick.

'Really? Well that used to be the Doctor's house and surgery at one time. Up to 1947, I believe. There's a photograph of it somewhere – have a look on the wall over there. I'm a newcomer, only lived here nine years. But many of the villagers have lived here all their lives. Someone would remember, I'm sure.'

They scanned the wall. Old grainy photos, sepia-coloured and black and white, of Sunday school outings, miners and mines, the railway station, the old High Street with women in long dresses, the village school and its children...and suddenly there it was. The front garden was blooming. A board announced *To the Surgery* and an arrow pointed to the side of the house. The side path could be seen clearly, and the glimpse of a porch. 'There *was* a door,' thought Laura. 'Where I saw those steps. The back room must have been the surgery.'

An old-fashioned car, its hood down, was parked on the road outside. Sitting at the wheel, looking at the camera sat a man with a moustache, wearing a hat. Beneath it a label said, 'Storrington Surgery circa 1912' and 'Dr P. Kimber'. At the top of the display, a card announced, 'All photographs kindly loaned by Mrs Quigley.'

*

187

'Come on,' said Nick, hurrying out.

'We can't,' said Laura. 'Not after the other day – I couldn't face her. Anyway – you said she was a loony.'

'You can't be scared – not of an old woman,' said Nick.

'Just because she's got a photo of the house doesn't mean she knows anything about it, though.'

There was a distant rumble in the sky. Several large drops of rain darkened the pavement.

'She'll only scream at us – she'll recognise us for sure,' Laura added.

'She's all we've got to go on at the moment,' said Nick.

A vivid flash lit the sky, then a clap of thunder. The heavy drops became a torrent. They ran.

'We'll have to leave it for now!' shouted Nick. 'Quick – let's get home.'

Chapter Eighteen

*An oppressive highly charged atmosphere is often
a sign of a distressed spirit.*

THE HANDBOOK OF HAUNTINGS

They sat with trays on their laps as the video played before them on the screen. Laura watched without seeing. For ever after, the sight of spring rolls would remind her of this strange birthday. Outside it was as dark as a winter's evening. Wind and rain battered the windows.

'I'll be glad when the central heating's finished,' said Mrs Logan as she carried in the cake. 'Sarah made this, didn't you? She melted the chocolate and whipped the cream. What else did we put in it, Sarah?'

Sarah gave a vague shrug as if she couldn't remember.

'She's not herself at all, are you, love?' said Mrs Logan testing Sarah's forehead. 'It's odd – her temperature's down, not up. I'll take her to the doctor tomorrow, if she hasn't perked up.'

By the end of the film, an oppressive chill seemed to have invaded the house. Laura looked at them all. Even her parents appeared to be touched by it. Her mother tugging her cardigan, sagging against the cushions. Her father lifting his glasses and massaging between his eyes.

189

'I think we could all do with an early night,' sighed Mrs Logan.

Despite Sadie's absence, the sense of her in their room lingered. Nick's lamp was still on. He got out of bed and closed the door, then crossed to Sarah's bed. 'She's asleep already.'

'She's barely awake when she is awake – it's as if she's fading away,' said Laura.

The fact that Sadie had not reappeared only heightened her anxiety.

'D'you think she'll come tonight?' Nick asked.

Laura made a feeble 'Don't know' face.

'Perhaps she's here now,' he said looking round the room. 'Are you, Sadie? Come to see if we've found Gus yet? Can you hear me? Come on – speak up.'

Laura laughed. It took her by surprise. She felt she shouldn't, but watching Nick peering round the room, talking to the walls, she was overcome by uncontrollable laughter.

'Who's off this planet now?' she giggled. Then she had the urge to cry. She swallowed hard, holding it back.

'We can't stay awake all night,' she said. 'And even if we did – there's not much we can do, is there?'

Nick, deep in thought, didn't answer.

'You know, Nick, Sadie was different today – not so sure of herself. That song she was singing – it was so sad. It gave me the creeps.'

Nick looked at her. 'I still think we ought to try talking to her.'

'You try then, it didn't get me anywhere. But then she doesn't like me.'

Nick sat up, then, addressing the four corners of the room, spoke.

'Listen, Sadie, we're going to try and find Gus for you – like we said. That's what you want, isn't it? Then all your waiting will be over. You'll be happy again – and you can go. But while we're looking for Gus – you've got to leave Sarah alone. You're making her ill. Do you understand? She needs to sleep. To be herself. Leave her alone. OK?'

They sat waiting in the stillness, hoping for some sort of answer, glancing into the dark corners beyond the reach of the dim light. After a minute, Nick said, 'Perhaps I could write a note – in case she comes and we're both asleep. Do you think she can read?'

'According to Sarah, she can spell rhinoceros,' said Laura, reaching for her pad and pen.

'I don't believe I'm doing this,' Nick said as he wrote. 'Talking and writing letters to the dead. I'm not dreaming this, am I? There – that's pretty much what I just said. I'll stick it on Sarah's bed.'

'Better not let Mum or Dad see it,' said Laura.

'We ought to take turns in staying awake – just in case,' said Nick. 'Who's going first?'

'I can't sleep anyway,' said Laura.

She pulled a sweatshirt from her chair, tugged it over her nightshirt and propped herself up on her pillows. Nick's tossing and turning told her that he wasn't getting much sleep either. He looked over his shoulder at her.

'We're going to have to think what to do if we can't—' He stopped mid-sentence, remembering that Sadie could be listening. 'You know...' he said slowly, 'if Mrs Quigley really is a witch, she might know what to do. Or maybe it's something to do with her already. Conjuring things up that should be left alone. I mean – how did she know your name?'

Thanks a lot, Nick, thought Laura.

She sat in the half-dark, trying not to imagine things. The lamp cast shadows which she shut her eyes against. Nick was still now. She could hear the rain against the glass. The darkness seemed to intensify, to wrap itself around her, to smother her. She could see the railway embankment again – in the distance. She's running towards it through the rain, rivulets of water streaming down her face, soaking through to the skin. Panting for breath, throat aching, chest heaving from running. A strong smell of wet sooty earth and the hot smell of oil and iron and smoke. Climbing the bank in a desperate hurry, slipping, sliding back in the mud. At the top at last. Something huge and black – an enormous black engine, hissing steam. And men, running, shouting, calling. Running towards her and shouting. Voices everywhere. Arms grabbing her – dragging her away. But it's too late – too late – she has seen. Seen the white bows, pounded by rain into rags in the mud. The blue dress – no longer blue. And the small body on the glistening, black rail. The shiny black shoe beneath the engine's wheel. And the things she does not want to see...

She hears herself scream... '*No-o-o-o-o-o-o*!'

Jolting awake. A strange woman stands by her bed

looking down at her. Her face a pale mask of pain and grief. And accusation. Unbearable – unbearable. The woman leans over her...

'It's all right Laura, just a nightmare. Don't think about it...'

Her mother, in her nightdress, was leaning over her, pushing back her hair. Her father stood next to her, yawning. Nick was somehow over by Sarah's bed. Sarah blinked sleepily at everyone.

'Well, what was that all about?' said her father, scratching his head.

'Don't ask her, Don. It's worse if she talks about it. Just forget it, Laura. It's only a bad dream. Put it out of your mind – that's the best way, Laura love.'

Her mother patted the pillows and straightened the bed.

'I didn't think anyone could scream that loud,' whispered Nick when they'd gone. 'I practically hit the ceiling. What happened?'

'Is Sarah all right?' Laura asked quietly.

They lay still in the darkness.

'Yeah – she's gone back to sleep. I had to whip that note off pretty quick.'

'I don't want her to hear this, Nick,' she said. 'I was Gus again. I know how Sadie died. And I won't ever be able to forget it – whatever Mum says. She was killed, Nick! Killed by a steam engine! She must have been standing on the track when it hit her. Oh Nick – I can still see it – I wish I couldn't! It was terrible, Nick, just terrible...'

When she'd finished, Nick was quiet.

'Do you think maybe Gus is dead and he's haunting you?' he asked. 'Perhaps he's trying to get in touch with Sadie through you – to say he's sorry or something.'

'It's like I'm reliving it. Is that possible? This was Gus's room, you know. Does that make sense?'

'No. But then none of this makes sense.'

Laura heard him sigh.

'I suppose it does sort of fit together though, doesn't it?' he said after a while. 'Let's say Gus took Sadie to his den or whatever. Then he goes off, telling her to wait there. Sadie gets fed up and goes looking for him. Climbs bank. Crosses railway line. Gets killed by steam engine. And if that's what happened there'd be some sort of record. There'd have been a report in the local paper for sure. At last! We've got something we can follow up. But first we'll see old Mrs Q – tomorrow morning. She may even know something about it.'

'I don't know how you can be so cold-blooded about it, Nick. You've got no idea – it was awful, Nick. Imagine seeing your sister like that. Imagine knowing that it was your fault. Imagine having to live with that. I'll never forget it. Never.'

Next morning Sarah was quieter than usual though not quite so droopy. But the heavy atmosphere of the house was still tangible. Laura and Nick tried to get her to go with them.

'I'm waiting for Sadie to come and play,' she said. 'But you mustn't tell Mummy or Daddy because I'm not allowed to talk about her.'

'Has she been here?' asked Laura.

Sarah shook her head. 'Not for ages. I thought I saw her – but then I fell asleep.'

Laura looked at Nick, then back to Sarah. 'Come on, Sarah – come with us – *please.*' She tried lifting Sarah from the floor where she was playing with a jigsaw.

'Don't want to. Leave me – leave me!' she screamed.

'Oh, do leave her alone, Laura!' snapped Mrs Logan, walking in.

'You'll have to go on your own,' said Nick.

'What? I can't...'

'Someone's got to stay here – with Sarah. You're the one who knows about Gus. You had the dreams – not me. Go on – you can do it. You stood up to Sadie, didn't you? She's just an old lady, that's all.'

Laura knew Nick was right, but it didn't make her feel any better. She gave a resigned but doubtful grimace. 'She'll probably slam the door in my face,' she told him. 'And I don't think I'd blame her really.'

She set off on her bike. The sky was clear but sunless, the pavements beginning to dry out, leaving puddles of leaves and debris in the gutters. As she reached the gate, Laura remembered the bony hands, the fierce face, the threat of 'I know you, Laura!' She blanked them out. Leaving her bike at the gate, she walked up the path.

She stood before Mrs Quigley's front door, reached out, lifted the knocker and rapped twice. From the corner of her eye, Laura saw a curtain move. She waited, listening and imagining all sorts of dreadful things. She made herself knock again. Still no answer. She bent and lifted the flap of the letterbox.

'Hello!' she called. 'Mrs Quigley? It's Laura, Laura Logan. I've come to apologise – for the other day. I'm very sorry if we were rude to you. And I need to ask you something. About our house. We saw your photos in the village hall – my brother Nick and me.'

She stepped back, then had second thoughts and called again. 'And I'd be very grateful, Mrs Quigley, if you could tell me about the house – and its history. Especially if you know anything about Sadie and Gus.'

She heard something move behind the door. Slowly it opened to a crack. There was a glimpse of red beret, and spikes of white hair. Two bright blue eyes, startling in such an old face, glared at Laura.

'Well?' the old woman demanded. 'Have you come to apologise or not?'

'I'm very sorry, Mrs Quigley,' said Laura hurriedly.

The eyes considered her piercingly.

She knew my name, thought Laura. Does she know what I'm thinking?

'Sadie and Gus, you said. Who are Sadie and Gus?'

'Their names are written on the back of a door – in the kitchen. A height chart – with dates,' Laura said.

The eyes held her.

'I wondered if you knew anything about them – we're interested in the history of the house, you see.'

The old woman glowered at Laura.

'What we're really trying to find out,' Laura gabbled, 'is what happened to Sadie – and to Gus – because it just stops, the height chart...' The door began to close.

'I'm busy – if you bother me again I shall call the police.'

'But, Mrs Quigley...'

It banged shut.

Damn, damn, damn! thought Laura. She turned to go. Then abruptly turned back and called through the letterbox, 'I want to know about Gus, Mrs Quigley – if he's still alive. It's very important. I know that Sadie got killed – on the old railway line – and Gus was there and saw it...'

There was a tiny movement behind the door. Then it opened.

'Is this another of your silly games?' the old woman barked.

Laura felt fixed by her eyes. Like a moth on a pin.

Then suddenly Mrs Quigley said, 'I am not particularly fond of children. But you'd better come inside. Wipe your feet.'

Laura took a deep breath and followed her into a room. She stopped and stared. A tiger stared at her from behind grasses. The beady eye of a parrot gleamed from a high branch. Fantastic birds displayed exotic plumage. Creepers, brilliantly coloured flowers, leaves dripped and trailed. A lizard climbed a trunk. A toad squatted in the shade of a giant leaf. Vivid butterflies fluttered. Snakes twined. Every wall and surface had been painted with scenes of a tropical paradise. There were living plants too, climbing the walls, and winding along the dark beams above them. It was not easy to tell what was real and what was illusion. Eyes peered at her from the shady depths. The eyes that Shane's brother had reported staring at him.

Mrs Quigley pointed to a shabby sofa. Laura squeezed herself between some piles of papers and old-looking books, perching on the edge.

'Well? Explain!' the old woman ordered, easing herself into an armchair.

Laura noticed that the old woman wore a vivid purple shirt and orange trousers under her old brown coat.

'It's hard to explain,' said Laura. 'It's not just the height chart you see. It really started the day we moved in...'

She hadn't intended to mention any of this. Only to find out about Gus and Sadie. But for some reason, she felt compelled to tell her everything.

'Our little sister – that's Sarah – said she'd made a friend – and her name was Sadie. She met her in the garden, she said. She had long black plaits and a blue dress and shiny black shoes—'

Mrs Quigley's hand gripped the side of the armchair. 'Stop, child, stop. Now start again – slowly.'

Once she had started, Laura couldn't stop. It all flooded out, sometimes out of order, then she would remember something she'd left out and interrupt herself. 'She kept singing this song, "Sadie, beautiful Sadie".' From time to time, Laura would glance up to see if Mrs Quigley was still listening and she would wave her on.

'And then there were these weird dreams – like I was Gus.'

Mrs Quigley listened intently in silence.

'And we think that's why Sadie's still here – and that if Gus was still alive, then he might be able to help – and then she could go,' said Laura when at last she had finished.

Mrs Quigley sat with her eyes closed. After a moment she opened them. She looked distressed. 'Would you get me a drink of water, please? Through there.' She pointed to a door.

Laura went to the kitchen. The walls here were covered in paintings too. An orchard of fruit trees against pale cloud-scudding skies, apples and peaches and plums, but also strange fruits that she had never seen before. Great bunches of dark drying leaves hung from the ceiling beams, like sleeping bats. The window ledge was crammed with potted plants, filtering the light like a forest. Above the sink were shelves crammed with small bottles and jars. Laura squinted at them. Some glistened with dark liquids. Here were long seed-like objects, there dry curling leaves, some writhing stringy coils and...Laura stepped back...white fleshy lumps.

She hurriedly filled a cup from the tap and took it to Mrs Quigley. She waited while she sipped slowly. At last, she put down the cup and said, 'The answer to your question is, yes. Gus is still alive. I am Gus.'

Chapter Nineteen

Death is certain. What is uncertain, is what lies beyond.
THE HANDBOOK OF HAUNTINGS

'But Gus is – was – a boy!' insisted Laura.

The merest hint of a smile fluttered on the old woman's lips.

'Wanted to be. Dressed like one most of the time – much to my parents' irritation. My name is Augustina. Quite fond of it now, but hated it as a girl. Called myself Gus – wouldn't answer to anything else at home. Haven't been called that for years – my husband called me Tina—' She broke off.

'All this time...' she said to herself. 'All this time. Poor child, poor child...' She closed her eyes and pressed her fingers against them.

'You believe me, then?' said Laura.

'Of course – yes, yes.' The old woman nodded as if to herself. 'That song – our father used to sing it to her...'

'But why didn't you ever *see* her?'

'Did *you* see her?' demanded Mrs Quigley.

Laura shook her head.

'I am not a psychic,' the old woman went on. 'Your little sister Sarah clearly is. A natural sensitive – a medium.

Not that she knows it – yet. But I'm familiar with such things. It's a rare gift.'

'But Sadie said she couldn't find you,' said Laura.

'I was sent away – almost immediately – to an aunt. Then to school. My mother never forgave me. I've never forgiven myself. It was my fault, you see.' Mrs Quigley closed her eyes again. 'Shortly afterwards, my father retired and sold the practice. He was much older than my mother.'

'Dr Kimber,' said Laura. 'So it all happened – just like my dreams?'

The old woman nodded. 'You know, they carried Sadie back to the house – to my father's surgery. I followed, running after them. I can still see my father's face. And my mother's when she came to see what all the commotion was about...' her voice trailed off. She eased herself from her chair. 'We must hurry,' she said. 'What do your parents know of all this?'

Laura told her.

'Then we best leave them out of it,' she said. 'It would not be an easy matter to convince them. They'll take me for a crazy old woman. I'm used to that – but we cannot afford to waste time. So I'll not come to the house.'

'What are you going to do?'

'We'll go to the railway. You must get Sarah out of the house and bring her along. We shall need her.'

'But it's the house that she haunts,' said Laura, getting up.

'It's where she waited and where she died,' said Mrs Quigley sharply. 'And I imagine it's where she still waits from time to time.' She rummaged in a drawer and slipped something into her pocket. Together they left the house.

'Sadie was not a wicked child, you know,' she told Laura as they hurried along, Laura pushing her bike. 'Each of us has good and bad within us. But now she is a lost child. A lost spirit. Alone and confused. And frightened. In that condition there is no telling what she might do. Evil feeds on fear you know. It slowly destroys innocence. Some of that innocence still remains – or Sarah would not still be Sarah. All Sadie has at the moment is Sarah – and her powerful hold over her. Sarah is too young to block her – to shut her out. But she will learn to do such things in time. Meanwhile, she is in danger. You are right to be worried, Laura.'

Laura looked at the old woman. At her white hair, at her bony hands, the veins like strings. So different from the Gus she thought she knew. Mrs Quigley caught her eye.

'Not what you expected, I imagine.'

'You can say that again,' thought Laura. 'But how did I dream all that – I don't understand,' she said.

'I've been asking myself that question, Laura,' said Mrs Quigley. 'I saw you on the day you moved in, you know. You were chasing your sister, making her scream. I heard your father shout at you – none too pleased he sounded. And suddenly I was a child again. It reminded me of myself – and Sadie – and that house. Some things you can never forget. They won't go away – even when you tell them to. Others you welcome. When you get to my age, the past sometimes seems more vivid than the present. Charlie Maggs – that's who I was going to meet. One of the carting boys at the mine. My parents would have been appalled if they knew. Used to meet up in our den. Only in the summer – those boys didn't see daylight in winter, except on Sundays, their day off. He gave me a lucky rabbit's foot and I...' Mrs Quigley seemed to be lost in thought, staring into the distance. She paused, then looked at Laura.

'Then one day, Sadie made me take her along. I didn't want to. So I left her in the den – told her to wait. Made her promise. And I went off to meet Charlie. She didn't know about Charlie – I meant to keep it that way. And – I forgot all about her. She must have gone looking. You know what happened. It was such a dreadful thing – so dreadful...' She stared fiercely ahead.

'So – was I picking up those memories from you?' asked Laura.

Mrs Quigley didn't answer straight away.

'I believe we leave something of ourselves behind – wherever we go,' she said at last. 'Particularly strong emotions. They leave their own electrical energy. Perhaps you plugged into those – the highly charged emotions from when I was a child in that room – I couldn't say. I was quite a solitary child – spent a good deal of my time that room. Happy times – and painful times.'

'I found your old hiding place,' Laura told her.

Mrs Quigley looked puzzled.

'In the cupboard – under the floorboard.'

'The loose floorboard,' said Mrs Quigley slowly. 'Yes, yes – I'd forgotten all about that.'

'Your tobacco tin's still there,' said Laura.

*

204

Mrs Quigley said she would wait in the porch of the church. Laura found Sarah and Nick in the kitchen. Nick was helping Sarah make a picture out of glue and fabric scraps, while their mother sat at her sewing machine making curtains. A look of relief quickly followed by one of query crossed Nick's face. She tried to signal the urgent need to get Sarah away.

'Where have you been?' said her mother irritably. 'I could have done with some help this morning.'

Already Laura sensed the tension of the house seeping into her. Sarah crossly pushed her gluey picture away. She got down and pressed her face against the window, peering down the garden.

'This is boring,' said Nick, looking at Laura and standing up. 'Oi, Sarah. How about going down to the park then?'

Sarah sighed and shook her head slowly. Several other suggestions met with equal indifference. Their mother glanced at them. Laura looked at her watch. Nearly twelve minutes since she'd left Mrs Quigley. Then, suddenly inspired, she snatched a wide strip of fabric from the floor and said, 'Hey, Sarah, we could make something for Prudence from this. Come on – let's see.' She grabbed the pig from the table and ran upstairs.

Sarah peeled herself from the window and followed. Nick, aware of his mother's curiosity, delayed, helping himself to a biscuit and feigning interest in her curtains, which only made her more suspicious.

'Shut the door,' ordered Laura when he got upstairs.

Nick didn't get a chance to ask what had happened.

'Sarah says Sadie's been here,' Laura burst. 'Is that right?'

'I dunno,' Nick shrugged. 'All I know is she kept looking out of the window – I couldn't get her out of there. I'm almost dead from boredom.'

'She's being horrible to me,' Sarah complained. 'She just looks at me and stares and stares.'

'Where is she now?' Nick demanded, looking round.

'She was in the garden. She keeps looking at me through the window. Then she goes. Then she comes. And then she goes. And I wanted to play.'

Nick looked at Laura. 'Perhaps it's a good sign,' he suggested. 'Perhaps she saw our note or heard us. I mean – she's leaving her alone, isn't she? That's what we asked, isn't it?'

'Let's hope so,' Laura muttered. But it did little to lessen her anxiety. Even if Nick was right, it was clear Sadie was becoming impatient. Mrs Quigley's words, 'Evil feeds on fear', echoed in her head. She had wasted too much time already.

'Listen, Sarah,' said Laura, kneeling down, 'I need you to come with me.'

'But you said you were going to make something for Prudence – she wants some shorts – can you make some shorts for her, Laura?' she asked, winding the fabric around the pig's legs.

'Yes, yes,' agreed Laura. 'Later – but I've got something to tell you.'

She stood up and looked at Nick. 'I've found Gus.'

'What!' Nick exploded.

'Where?' said Sarah, suddenly interested.

'Waiting for us at the church. And now we've got to find Sadie to tell her. We can't waste time, Nick! Are you sure she's not here, Sarah?' she asked.

Sarah went to the window and peered down. 'Nope.'

'Come on then.' She took Sarah's hand.

'Where?' said Sarah.

'Hold on, hold on!' demanded Nick. 'What's happening? Where did you find him? What happened?'

'I haven't got time to explain, Nick. Come on!' She headed for the door.

Sarah stood frowning. 'I want to wait here for Sadie.'

Laura groaned with exasperation.

'Listen Sarah – perhaps Sadie's too sad to play. We asked Sadie to leave you alone, Sarah. So we could find Gus. She's doing what we asked. It was making you ill and tired, you see.'

'But I wanted to play,' said Sarah.

'Come on,' said Laura, taking her hand. 'We'll go and find her then. We'll tell Mum we're going to the park,' she told Nick.

'You didn't say Mrs Quigley was here too,' said Nick as he caught side of the old woman sitting inside the church porch. 'Where's Gus – is he inside?'

'Mrs Quigley – this is Sarah. And this is my brother Nick,' Laura panted.

'I think I know your brother – and his friend,' observed Mrs Quigley.

'Nick, Sarah...' Laura took a big breath. 'This is Gus.'

Nick's face went through various contortions. His mouth moved but made no sound.

Sarah stared at the old woman, her mouth open. 'No it isn't,' she said. 'Gus isn't an old lady.'

'I haven't always been so old you know,' said Mrs Quigley. 'But, believe me, a long time ago, when I was a little girl, I was called Gus – and Sadie was my little sister.'

Sarah frowned, unconvinced. From her pocket, Mrs Quigley withdrew an old sepia-coloured photograph. 'Look – I brought this to show you.'

It was a family photo. A man and a woman, seated. On the man's lap, a beautiful little girl in a white dress, stockings and shoes. Her luxurious dark hair rippled over her shoulders, a huge bow at the top, a deep fringe. Standing beside them a tall awkward skinny girl, her hair cropped short, looking as if she didn't want to be there.

'There's Sadie,' cried Sarah, pointing at the girl with the bow.

'Yes – and there's me,' said Mrs Quigley. 'And our father and mother.'

Laura felt a small shiver. The mother was the pale-faced woman who had stood so accusingly beside her bed.

Mrs Quigley took Sarah's hand. 'Do you understand, Sarah? Sadie died.'

Sarah nodded. 'No one can see her except me – I'm special.'

'You are indeed – very special,' said Mrs Quigley. 'And we need your help. Sadie shouldn't be here any more. We have to help her – to move on.'

'Where will she go?' said Sarah.

'To the next part of her journey – where she should be. Will you help us? It may make you feel very sad – but you're the only one who can see and hear her. Come along then.'

They stood at the top of the embankment, fields and scrub on either side, Mrs Quigley breathing heavily from the walk and the climb. Laura had only managed to give Nick the briefest account of what had taken place at her house.

After a moment Mrs Quigley said, 'Sarah, you must hold my hand, and Laura's too. Laura, hold Nick's hand. Don't let go unless I tell you. Now I need to find my bearings.' She scanned her surroundings. 'As near to the place she died as possible,' she said, setting off again.

They stopped several times while Mrs Quigley searched for a landmark she recognised. She hesitated again, then walked a little further.

'It's all so different now,' she said to herself.

A scattering of cows grazed in the distance. An aeroplane passed overhead. It's too ordinary, too normal, thought Laura. Thank goodness no one's here – we must look really cranky. Nick was looking distinctly uncomfortable.

'What's going to happen?' Nick asked Mrs Quigley.

'That remains to be seen. Nothing is certain – we may be wasting our time. But we must hold on to Sarah. We must not put her at risk. Spirits do not like being constrained. If Sadie attempts to repossess the child – do not let go!'

Mrs Quigley was watching Sarah carefully as they

moved slowly forward. Suddenly Sarah recoiled as if she had hit a wall of glass. She stumbled back, then looked up at them.

'Did you see that? Sarah has sensed something – this is the cold spot,' said the old woman. 'This is where it happened – where Sadie died. I've seen this before, but never in one so young. She's a true psychic.' She put a hand to her forehead. 'I'm so sorry – it brings it all back you see...'

Laura could feel Sarah's hand tighten. Mrs Quigley was alert to it too. Sarah was staring as if in a trance, her face pale. Staring down, shaking her head.

'Sad – so sad – so sad...' It sounded like a whimper. 'She's all hurt – and she can't get up – and the men are shouting and she's all wet – all wet and...' Sarah was distressed, turning her head, trying not to look, pulling away.

'Don't look, Sarah,' Mrs Quigley commanded gently. 'Look up, look up! You're only seeing what happened here many years ago. That's not Sadie now – she's not hurt any more. Look for the real Sadie. Can you see her? Call her, Sarah.'

'Sadie! Sadie!' Sarah called.

An intense silence descended on them as if they were enclosed in a glass dome, cut off from the world.

'Look – there she is! She's not hurt now! Look!' cried Sarah.

The others looked and saw nothing. Mrs Quigley stood erect, staring fiercely ahead. She glanced down at Sarah. She saw, as Laura and Nick could see, Sarah's face crumple.

'What's the matter, Sarah?' Laura whispered.

'She says she hates me – I'm not her friend any more – and she hates you and Nick. 'Cos you tell lies and she's going to teach us all a lesson...'

'Stop!' ordered Mrs Quigley. 'Listen to me, Sadie. No one has lied to you. I'm here, Sadie. Look at me – it's Gus...'

Suddenly Laura felt her arms being wrenched and twisted. Sarah writhed and squirmed, trying to tear herself away. Laura saw the alarm on Mrs Quigley's face.

'Hold her, Laura!' she cried. 'Sadie's trying to take her! Whatever happens – do not let go! Nick! Help us!'

Nick let go of Laura's hand and made a grab for the girl. She fought and kicked with the strength and ferocity of a wild animal. She hissed and snarled at Nick. Quite suddenly, she stopped. Then without warning, lashed out with her foot, kicking him in the face, sending him backwards. Laura was holding on with both hands now. Suddenly Mrs Quigley gave a cry and staggered back as the girl landed a kick on her shin. Nick lunged again, just as the girl sunk her teeth into Laura's hand. With a scream, Laura let go. The girl darted away. She turned and laughed.

'You'll never catch me. You can catch Sarah, but not me. And if you hurt me – you'll hurt Sarah. You can't get rid of me. Not ever.'

They stood helpless, watching her. Mrs Quigley signalled with her hand, as if to say, 'Stay where you are.'

'Sadie,' she called.

'Shut up! Shut up! Shut your stupid mouth! You ugly old woman!' the girl spat.

Mrs Quigley started to sing. '*Sadie, beautiful Sadie...*'

Her voice was cracked and trembling. The girl's eyes narrowed.

'Remember that song?' called Mrs Quigley quietly. 'Remember how Daddy used to sing it to you. And how Mummy brushed your hair. Your beautiful hair. One hundred strokes every night.'

The girl watched and waited.

'Remember this, Sadie?' said Mrs Quigley. From her pocket she withdrew a gold heart-shaped locket on a chain. 'They gave it to you on your seventh birthday. And here they are inside.' The woman's old fingers picked at the clasp. She held it out: two tiny heart-shaped photos inside.

The girl took several steps forward.

'They loved you very much, Sadie. Do you remember what Gus gave you? I do. A painting of a tiger.'

The girl's expression of hate and anger was fading. She looked confused.

'Laura and Nick did not lie to you, Sadie,' the old woman went on. 'They kept their promise. They found Gus for you. I am Gus, Sadie.'

'No you're not!' the girl scowled.

'Yes, I am, Sadie. I'm old now – but here I am. This is where I told you to wait, remember? I made you promise. And you waited and waited. But I never came back. Till now. Here I am, Sadie. I've come back for you.' She lifted her hands to the girl.

For several seconds no one moved or spoke. Laura looked at the girl. How small and lost and alone she looked. No longer defiant. Or threatening.

'I'm here now, Sadie,' said Mrs Quigley softly. Her eyes were wet. 'And I'm sorry for leaving you here – for so long. Will you ever forgive me?'

The girl stepped slowly towards her. She stared at her. Then put her hands out to the old woman.

'I'm sorry – so sorry, Sadie,' said Mrs Quigley, taking her hands. 'You don't need to wait any longer, Sadie. You kept your promise. You are free now – and you must go. But first you must give Sarah back to us.'

The girl stared up at the old woman's face, saying nothing. An intense feeling of terrible sadness seeped into them all. Quite suddenly, she went limp. Mrs Quigley caught her as Laura and Nick rushed forward.

'Good – we have Sarah back,' she sighed. 'Look after her. We haven't finished yet. Thank you, Sadie. Now we can help you,' she said.

Laura and Nick held on to Sarah. She was confused, unsteady and drowsy, but she nodded when Mrs Quigley bent and asked, 'Sarah? Can you hear me? Where is Sadie now, Sarah?'

Sarah blinked. 'Just there.' She pointed a few feet away.

Mrs Quigley straightened. Addressing the spot that Sarah had pointed to, she said, 'You kept your promise, Sadie. You are a good girl for keeping your promise. You are a good girl for giving Sarah back. But I'm here now – and you don't have to wait any longer. You are free. You must look for the light, Sadie. Do you see the light? Look for it – look for it – look for the light. And follow it, Sadie. Follow the light...' Mrs Quigley's face was folded in concentration.

The four of them waited, separated by silence. Sarah's eyes fixed on something far away. Laura, Nick and Mrs Quigley watched her.

'What's happening?' Nick whispered to Laura.

'What do you see, Sarah?' Mrs Quigley asked gently.

'There it is,' said Sarah in quiet wonder. 'There! Over there!' She pointed excitedly. 'A light – a little white light! It's growing – it's getting bigger and bigger – and Sadie's looking at it. And there's a man – it's the man in the picture – and there's the lady too – they're waiting – for Sadie. They're waving to her – to come. And Sadie's seen them – she's running – she's going... Oh, she's going...'

They stood. For how long, Laura couldn't tell. Time seemed to have stopped. Sarah watching something none of them could see. Laura and Nick waiting and watching Sarah and the old woman.

Suddenly, a pair of pigeons fluttered from a nearby tree and flapped above them, startling Laura. The invisible dome surrounding them dissolved. The world seemed full of sound. Of trees rustling, of birds twittering, of their shoes against the path.

'It's gone,' said Sarah sadly. 'They've all gone.'

Mrs Quigley looked exhausted and very old. She bent her head, closed her eyes as if the children weren't there. Then, abruptly, she straightened up.

'Well done, Sarah. Well done.' She laid her hand on Sarah's head.

Laura looked at Sarah. Her expression was calm, unfazed by her extraordinary experience. Still looking with wonder into the distance.

'Thank you, Sarah,' Mrs Quigley continued. 'You've helped Sadie – and me too. Now, if you can all manage the walk, you must come home with me. There are things you should all understand.'

Chapter Twenty

We should not be afraid of ghosts. They are, after all,
evidence of life after death.

THE HANDBOOK OF HAUNTINGS

Mrs Quigley sat them down then sank wearily into her chair. Nick and Sarah gazed in awe around the walls of the room.

'So, Nick – you still have doubts, I think,' said Mrs Quigley.

He shrugged. 'It doesn't make sense – any of it.'

'And what about you, Laura?' she asked.

'I'm worried about Sarah – whether she understands all this. I don't – not really. It's sort of scary.'

'Yeah – it's big stuff this,' said Nick. 'Life and death – and all that.'

'When do you think life begins?' asked Mrs Quigley.

'I dunno – when you're born, I suppose,' said Nick.

'And before that?'

He shrugged again.

'Would it frighten you – the notion that you existed before you were born?'

Laura shook her head. Nick said, 'No – why?'

'Then why be anxious about the possibility that you continue after you die?'

'But what would have happened if Sadie hadn't gone? And what would have happened to Sarah?' asked Laura.

Mrs Quigley nodded.

'I believe good will always outweigh evil,' she said. 'In the end.'

'But what if we hadn't found you?' said Laura.

'You would have looked for help elsewhere. There are others, far more expert than I, who could have helped you. I'm sure you would have persevered till you found someone, Laura.' She stood up. 'I need a cup of tea,' she said. 'I think we could all do with a drink. Sarah – you can help me. Have you ever tasted elderflower cordial?'

From where they sat, Laura and Nick could hear the murmur of voices from the kitchen. But not what was being exchanged.

'Anyway – Sadie's gone. Thank goodness it's all over,' said Nick to Mrs Quigley as she handed him a glass.

Mrs Quigley eyed him shrewdly. 'I doubt that,' she said. 'I doubt that very much indeed.'

'What? You don't mean she'll come back?' he spluttered.

'No. Sadie has gone. But your young sister here has a special gift.' She nodded towards Sarah. '*That* won't go away. It is her you must watch. Laura, I think, understands that already. Do *you* understand?' she asked Nick. 'It is a gift. But it's also a burden.' She turned to Laura. 'And perhaps you too, Laura, are sensitive – to some lesser extent. Your dreams were extraordinarily accurate.'

'But I thought that was something to do with the room.'

'Yes. But only *you* tuned into that energy,' said Mrs Quigley. 'Not Nick, or Sarah.'

'Sarah?' She turned to the little girl perched on the sofa.

Sarah took her gaze from the walls and looked at Mrs Quigley.

'You are able to see and hear things that most of us cannot see or hear – you know that, don't you?'

Sarah nodded. 'Mummy and Daddy didn't believe me. Or Nick. They thought Sadie was pretend.'

'There will always be people who don't believe you,' Mrs Quigley said. 'But as you grow up you will learn how to deal with that. And also how to use your special gift. At the moment it is only a seed. But it will grow and flower. However, sometimes you will need to protect yourself – to pretend too. It would be best, I think, if you said nothing to your mother and father about today – or what I've told you. Not yet. They will not understand. I shall try and help explain to them at some stage. The time will come when they will have to accept it. Now – before you go...' She sat down at a small table, took a sheet of paper from a drawer, wrote, then folded it and sealed it in an envelope. She turned to Laura and Nick. 'You must both take care of her,' she said. 'You see how tiring it is for her? And things are not over. For Sarah they are only just beginning.' She stood up wearily and held the envelope out to Laura. 'Keep this in a safe place, Laura. Should the time come when you need help again, then you may open it.'

*

'What was she saying to you?' Nick asked Sarah as they walked home.

Sarah shook her head. 'She said you'd ask me. She said I had to say you wouldn't understand.'

'Do *you* understand, Sarah?' said Laura.

'I just *know*,' said Sarah.

All three of them were in a quiet and thoughtful mood by the time they reached home. Laura, free of Sadie, felt spent. But with a sense of relief so strong she wanted to laugh and cry at the same time.

'Be sure of one thing,' Mrs Quigley had told them as they left. 'Things will never be the same again.'

The moment they entered the house, Laura felt the change. Something had shifted, lifted, lightened. Ordinary things seemed sharper, brighter. The redness of the tomatoes in the bowl, the green stars of their stalks. She wondered if Nick felt it too. He was unusually silent.

'Where have you been? I was getting worried about you,' their mother said.

'Out and about,' said Nick.

There was a postcard waiting for Laura on the table. It had a picture of a Welsh girl in a tall black hat and a shawl, sitting on a mountainside. She turned it over.

Happy birthday and all that. Prezzie later.
I have seen 5 castles, some rocks and rain,
rain, rain, rain.   Luv Nat.

You wouldn't believe what I've seen, thought Laura. No. Things will never be the same again. She went upstairs to their room and took from her pocket the envelope that Mrs Quigley had given to her. She held it up to the light, but she could see nothing through the thick parchment-like paper. She crossed to the cupboard and carefully hid it beneath the loose floorboard.

Laura, Nick and Sarah sat under the big tree in the garden.

'Sarah – what did you see exactly?' Laura asked.

'Yeah – all that bit about the light. What happened?' said Nick, pulling at the grass.

Sarah lay on her stomach, watching an ant labouring with a piece of leaf. She sat up and lifted Prudence on to her lap.

'It was so beautiful.' She blinked as if she could see it still. 'It was such a beautiful light – it made me want to go too. But I knew I couldn't. It made all the sadness go away and made me feel happy. And Sadie looked happy too. Then I was sad because it went away. And Sadie had gone.'

'Well, I didn't see anything,' said Nick. 'Not a thing.'

A few days later, at dinner time, Laura announced, 'From now on I want to be called Laurie – instead of Laura. I like names that could be male or female – it's more interesting,' she explained.

'Oh no – let's not start that again,' said her father. 'It was bad enough with Sarah and Sadie.'

Chewing his food, Nick looked at her, but said nothing.

'You said Sadie, Daddy,' Sarah told him. 'You said you never wanted to hear it again – and now you've said it.'

'Well – let that be the last time,' her father said.

'Anyway, Sadie's gone now,' said Sarah.

'I'm delighted to hear it,' he nodded.

'And I don't want wallpaper in my room after all, Mum,' Laura said. 'I'm going to paint my walls – with plants and birds and...'

'Just like—' started Sarah.

Nick coughed. 'Just like a jungle,' he said.

'That sounds wonderful,' nodded her mother. 'I like that idea.'

'You know something,' said their father leaning back. 'We have actually managed an entire meal without squabbling, throwing food, refusing to eat or referring to ghosts and the slaughter of animals. This is quite an occasion. Congratulations.'

The cat flap clanked furiously. Mrs White appeared, dragging something heavy along the floor.

'Oh no,' said their mother.

'What is it?' said Sarah, making a face.

'It's a chicken,' said their father, peering down and poking it. 'Would you believe it – still in its plastic bag – and partially frozen too.'

'I'm not burying a frozen chicken,' said Nick.

'Won't catch me touching it,' said Laura. 'All those salmonella germs. Poor thing – it's terrible in those batteries.'

A week later, Laura moved into her new attic bedroom and Natalie came to stay. She and Laura painted her walls together.

'This house is brilliant,' said Natalie. 'You made it sound totally disgusting.'

'You didn't see it when we moved in, Nat. I'm not kidding – it was really spooky.'

'Yeah, what about that? You said there were ghosts or something?' asked Natalie.

'Did I? Oh yeah. Well – when the bathroom's covered in green slime and there's stains like blood running down the walls and giant spider webs, and footsteps on the stairs – and when you look – there's no one there...' She shuffled towards Natalie in a floaty ghost-like way.

Natalie screamed. 'Stop it Laura! I'll have nightmares now!'

'What's happened to you? You're different,' Natalie told her later.

'How?' said Laura, studying her face in the mirror.

'I don't know – just different.'

Yeah, I feel different, Laura thought. But how could she explain to Natalie what had happened? As Mrs Quigley said, how could anyone else understand?

And later, nearly a year later, Mrs Quigley was proved right about something else. It wasn't all over. It was only just beginning.

NOT THE END

More Orchard Black Apples

All priced at £4.99

Orchard Black Apples are available from all good bookshops,
or can be ordered direct from the publisher:
Orchard Books, PO BOX 29, Douglas IM99 1BQ
Credit card orders: please telephone 01624 836000 or fax 01624 837033
or visit our Internet site: www.wattspub.co.uk
or e-mail: bookshop@enterprise.net for details.

To order please quote title, author and ISBN
and your full name and address.
Cheques and postal orders should be made payable to 'Bookpost plc.'
Postage and packing is FREE within the UK
(overseas customers should add £1.00 per book).
Prices and availability are subject to change.